V

SENDER: CLASSIFIED

SECURITY: FOR YOUR INFORMATION
READ AND DESTROY

RELAYED MESSAGE:

The SHEY GROUP is a private paramilitary organization headed by Logan Kincaid. These operatives take on high-risk, high-stakes missions in accord with U.S. government policy. All members are former CIA, FBI or military operatives with top-level security clearances and specialized skills. Members maintain close ties to the underground intelligence network and conduct high-level, behind-the-scenes operations for the government as well as private clients and corporations.

The U.S. government will disavow any connection to SHEY GROUP operations. Employ at your own risk.

Dear Harlequin Intrigue Reader,

It's the most wonderful time of the year! And we have six breathtaking books this month that will make the season even brighter....

THE LANDRY BROTHERS are back! We can't think of a better way to kick off our December lineup than with this long-anticipated new installment in Kelsey Roberts's popular series about seven rascally brothers, born and bred in Montana. In *Bedside Manner,* chaos rips through the town of Jasper when Dr. Chance Landry finds himself framed for murder...and targeted for love! Check back this April for the next title, *Chasing Secrets.* Also this month, watch for *Protector S.O.S.* by Susan Kearney. This HEROES INC. story spotlights an elite operative and his ex-lover who maneuver stormy waters—and a smoldering attraction—as they race to neutralize a dangerous hostage situation.

The adrenaline keeps on pumping with *Agent-in-Charge* by Leigh Riker, a fast-paced mystery. You'll be bewitched by this month's ECLIPSE selection—*Eden's Shadow* by veteran author Jenna Ryan. This tantalizing gothic unravels a shadowy mystery and casts a magical spell over an enamored duo. And the excitement doesn't stop there! Jessica Andersen returns to the lineup with her riveting new medical thriller, *Body Search,* about two hot-blooded doctors who are stranded together in a windswept coastal town and work around the clock to combat a deadly outbreak.

Finally this month, watch for *Secret Defender* by Debbi Rawlins—a provocative woman-in-jeopardy tale featuring an iron-willed hero who will stop at nothing to protect a headstrong heiress...even kidnap her for her own good.

Best wishes for a joyous holiday season from all of us at Harlequin Intrigue.

Sincerely,

Denise O'Sullivan
Senior Editor, Harlequin Intrigue

PROTECTOR S.O.S.

SUSAN KEARNEY

TORONTO • NEW YORK • LONDON
AMSTERDAM • PARIS • SYDNEY • HAMBURG
STOCKHOLM • ATHENS • TOKYO • MILAN • MADRID
PRAGUE • WARSAW • BUDAPEST • AUCKLAND

ISBN 0-373-22814-7

PROTECTOR S.O.S.

This edition published by arrangement with Harlequin Books S.A.

www.eHarlequin.com

Printed in U.S.A.

ABOUT THE AUTHOR

Susan Kearney used to set herself on fire four times a day; now she does something really hot—she writes romantic suspense. While she no longer performs her signature fire dive (she's taken up figure skating), she never runs out of ideas for characters and plots. A business graduate from the University of Michigan, Susan writes full-time. She resides in a small town outside of Tampa, Florida, with her husband and children, and a spoiled Boston terrier. Visit her at www.SusanKearney.com.

Books by Susan Kearney

HARLEQUIN INTRIGUE

340—TARA'S CHILD
378—A BABY TO LOVE
410—LULLABY DECEPTION
428—SWEET DECEPTION
456—DECEIVING DADDY
478—PRIORITY MALE
552—A NIGHT WITHOUT END
586—CRADLE WILL ROCK*
590—LITTLE BOYS BLUE*
594—LULLABY AND GOODNIGHT*
636—THE HIDDEN YEARS†
640—HIDDEN HEARTS†
644—LOVERS IN HIDING†
682—ROYAL TARGET**
686—ROYAL RANSOM**
690—ROYAL PURSUIT**
705—DADDY TO THE RESCUE††
709—DEFENDING THE HEIRESS††
713—SAVING THE GIRL NEXT DOOR††
774—OUT FOR JUSTICE
808—HIJACKED HONEYMOON††
814—PROTECTOR S.O.S.††

*The Sutton Babies
†Hide and Seek
**The Crown Affair
††Heroes Inc.

Dear Reader,

My HEROES INC. miniseries has been so popular that Harlequin has let me write more of them. Travis and Sandy's story in *Protector S.O.S.* was inspired by a genuine love of the sea. I have many fond memories of sailing during New Jersey summers, and while I have never encountered the kind of storm described in this book, I have a vivid imagination. Besides, pushing my characters to their limits, mentally, physically and emotionally is fun for me to write and, hopefully, will be a great read. I always enjoy hearing from my readers, and you can reach me through my Web site at www.SusanKearney.com.

Best,

Susan Kearney

CAST OF CHARACTERS

Travis Cantrel—Ex-Special Forces, currently employed by the Shey Group, Travis is accustomed to danger, but when he returns home to search for his kidnapped sister, his heart is in the most danger of all.

Sandy Vale—Travis's ex-lover, she now runs a marina and delivers sailboats with best friend and partner Ellie Cantrel.

Ellie Cantrel—Abducted by strangers, she never gives up hope of rescue. And meanwhile she wonders if Alan Lavelle is a friend or a foe.

Logan Kincaid—The leader of the Shey Group. He never hesitates to support the men who work for him.

Martin Vanderpelt—A mysterious and eccentric millionaire who has a plan—one that can endanger the entire eastern seaboard of the United States.

Alan Lavelle—A man with his own agenda.

Prologue

"You're late," Sandy Vale's eccentric millionaire client complained, his tone filled with annoyance, his wrinkled jowls sagging at his throat.

When Sandy and her first mate, Ellie Cantrel, delivered new sailboats to their buyers, most of them beamed from ear to ear. But not Martin Vanderpelt. He frowned, his lips pressed firmly together, as if he already knew that he would find something to complain about.

Sure that the cabin was shipshape, Sandy hopped off the deck, tied the bowline around the cleat on the dock, then straightened and tried to ignore Martin Vanderpelt's scowl. "We ran into a little rough weather, sir. Nothing your boat couldn't handle."

Ellie positioned bumpers between the boat and the

dock to protect the hull from scrapes, and Vanderpelt's glance lingered over Ellie's tanned legs. "For the money I paid, I expected your delivery to be on time."

"Sorry you had to wait, but I think you'll be pleased. She's a beauty, Mr. Vanderpelt." Sandy held out her hand in a friendly manner, pretending she didn't notice the coldness in Vanderpelt's expression. After a week at sea, she normally enjoyed landfall. But as clouds scudded over the sun and the air temperature dropped ten degrees, Vanderpelt ignored her handshake and climbed aboard the thirty-six-foot vessel, and Sandy wished she was back at sea.

She didn't like the way Vanderpelt had looked at Ellie. Not that lots of men didn't look at her friend. But something cold in his eyes warned her that he hadn't made all his millions by being a nice guy.

Reminding herself that Vanderpelt wasn't just any client and that she needed his goodwill, she bit back her sarcastic "So pleased to meet you, too." She couldn't afford to mouth off—not when he had bought a half dozen sailboats for his wealthy guests to race around the island. Despite the rumors about Vanderpelt's rude manners, Sandy and Ellie were hoping for repeat business. However, while they might not be chosen to deliver Vanderpelt's next boats, it would be worse if he complained about their service to the boat manufacturer who'd hired them.

Ellie and Sandy needed the extra money they earned delivering boats to help support their fledgling marina. Okay, maybe not so fledgling. They'd expanded over the last two years, adding a lucrative retail supply business to their main operation of leasing slips and selling fuel. They no longer worried over paying their bills, but they had more plans for expansion in the works.

Vanderpelt headed down below and Ellie rolled her smoky gray eyes at the sky, signaling what she thought of the high-and-mighty Vanderpelt. Sandy shrugged. During the past year, they'd had other unusual clients. A buyer in Florida had met them on his dock in his pajamas, a glass of champagne in his hand and a buxom blonde under each arm. A movie star in L.A. had burst into tears at the sight of his boat, totally overcome at finally being able to afford the yacht he'd always dreamed of. Sometimes Sandy felt like Santa Claus—but not today.

She distracted herself from Vanderpelt's displeasure by perusing his private island. Located about a hundred miles due east of Nova Scotia, and part of mainland Canada, the forbidding rocky shoreline and chain-link fence around the perimeter, with No Trespassing signs posted every ten feet, looked more like a military compound than the luxurious home of an eccentric millionaire.

A stately two-story house with a steeply pitched roof perched on tall pilings next to a clearing that looked like a helicopter pad. Vanderpelt's pilot was supposed to fly them back to Bar Harbor, Maine, where they could rent a car, head home and regroup before heading out to sea again.

Vanderpelt's thinning blond head poked out of the cabin, followed by the rest of him. Sandy had hoped his expression would have lightened to pleasure after seeing the rich mahogany cabinetry, the immaculate galley and the well-appointed cabin, decorated by a top Toronto designer.

But his blue eyes had narrowed, and the furrow between his brows had deepened to a fierce glower. "This is not my boat."

Sandy and Ellie exchanged "uh-oh" glances. Although Sandy's concern was intensifying with the storm blowing in, she kept her voice pleasant. "Mr. Vanderpelt. Lightning struck the mast of your boat and melted part of the hull. The manufacturer wanted you to have a brand-new, undamaged boat. You're lucky they had a replacement."

"You brought me a substitute? That's not good enough. It's unacceptable," he sputtered.

Sandy kept her tone businesslike to cover her annoyance. The customer wasn't supposed to know that his original boat had been damaged, and she was delivering a substitute, but obviously someone had screwed up either the design or the decor, clueing him in to the switch. "Sir, if you have a beef with the manufacturer, I suggest you call them. I'm a subcontractor. I was paid to deliver this boat to you. If the boat's unsatisfactory, you need to take that up with Danzler Marine. Not me."

"Damn right. You wait right here." Vanderpelt stalked off, his cheeks flushed with rage.

"Like we're going anywhere," Ellie muttered. "There's not another piece of land within a day's sail." She glanced at the dark cumulus clouds rolling in. "I think I'd prefer facing the storm and the sea to his mood."

"Hang on. We'll be out of here soon enough."

"I've got a bad feeling about him." Ellie shivered and glanced over her shoulder at Sandy, her usual dancing green eyes dimmed.

Sandy sighed. "I never understood why Danzler Marine didn't tell Vanderpelt up-front about the lightning, but now I know. They didn't want to deal with his temper." Sandy straightened her spine. "Keep in mind that he's so rich, he's probably accustomed to his every whim being catered to. When something goes wrong, he has all the self-restraint of a two-year-old."

Vanderpelt returned shortly with another man at his side. His cohort was about five foot ten, with dark, thinning hair, heavy-lidded eyes and pale skin that suggested he spent a lot of time indoors. His obsequious manner, and the duffel bag he carried, indicated he was an employee rather than a guest. As he blinked at them through his thick glasses, his bland face suggested to Sandy that the man was accustomed to Vanderpelt's rages. However, in contrast to his meek demeanor, his bulky jacket unnerved her.

"What's up?" Sandy asked, a lump of fear lodging in her gut. Ellie's brother, Travis, had worn jackets that bulged under the arm. Like Travis, this man was carrying a weapon. Unlike Travis, he had a shifty look to him. And the fact that Vanderpelt had brought muscle didn't bode well for Sandy and Ellie.

Vanderpelt raised his voice to be heard over the rising wind, the clanging halyards and the waves lashing the dock. "There's been a change of plans. Alan will return with you and make sure you bring back the one I ordered."

"Sorry, we don't take passengers." Sandy tried to politely refuse to take Alan.

Vanderpelt shook his head. "My agent at Danzler has agreed."

"Ellie and I can handle the job by ourselves. We sailed her here, we'll sail her back, together." And that couldn't be soon enough. Sandy untied the front cleat. As if reading her mind, Ellie started the engine.

That's when Alan drew his gun and aimed it at Ellie. He spoke with no inflection. "We're following Mr. Vanderpelt's orders. All of us."

He stepped aboard and motioned with his gun for Ellie to get under way. Eyes wide with fear, Ellie stared at Sandy, silently begging her to do something.

Oh…my…God. They were being hijacked at gunpoint. And there was not a damn thing Sandy could do about it.

Chapter One

"Travis? Travis? Damn it. Answer the phone." Travis Cantrel listened to his voice mail, but didn't need to wait for the caller to identify herself to recognize Sandy Vale's thick, Maine accent. It reminded him of lazy days at sea, erotic nights and stormy arguments. Odd, how they'd been so good in bed together, when the rest of the time all they'd done was fight. Travis hadn't heard from her in years. In fact, ever since their breakup eight years ago, the few times he'd been back home, Sandy had conveniently disappeared. His sister, Ellie, and Sandy were business partners at the rundown marina they'd bought, but, although he and Sandy had had no contact in close to a decade, her tone of voice told him she was in a panic.

"Travis, Ellie's in trouble. Get home. Now. And don't bring in the authorities. Whatever you do, don't do anything until we talk in person. Got to go."

Travis didn't wait to hear more. Although Sandy had called from a phone number he didn't recognize, he called her cell, his stomach rising up to his throat. Sandy never panicked. Hell, she didn't worry over the little stuff, or the big stuff. So if she was hysterical, Ellie must be… Had there been a car accident? Was Ellie sick? A million worries rushed through his head. Travis wasn't just Ellie's big brother. After their parents' deaths in a boating accident—he'd been twenty-two, Ellie seventeen—he'd been responsible for her. Sure, she was all grown up now. But as he stuffed clothing and toiletries into a suitcase, his pulse sped like a skidding race car about to slam into a wall.

Why the hell wasn't Sandy answering her phone? Why hadn't she told him what was wrong in her message?

Travis kept calling during the taxi ride to the Newark airport, where he could hop a commercial flight to Maine. After finishing a job in Alabama, he'd flown into New York City for some R and R and to visit his friend, Ryker Stevens. So he was free to pick up and go. Not that his boss, Logan Kincaid, would mind. Family came first, and Ellie was Travis's only family.

Travis called the Shey Group headquarters to let his boss know he was unavailable until further notice, and to ask for a trace on the phone Sandy had used. He found out the call had come from a pay phone in the back of a bar in the early hours of the morning. But why would she do that when she had a perfectly good cell phone?

Impatient for news, he called Sandy again just before his morning flight took off, and as soon as he landed at noon. He tried Ellie at home, at the marina and on her cell. No answer. Frantic, Travis rented a car and sped down the coast, cutting the two-hour drive to an hour and a half.

Normally he would have called the hospital, the police department, Ellie's other friends. But Sandy's warning made him wait. However, if Sandy and Ellie weren't at the Bayside Marina when he arrived, he would ask Kincaid and the Shey Group for help.

Travis slid to a stop in the gravel parking lot of Bayside Marina. The newly painted sign, the trimmed landscaping and the new roof made the old place look more upscale. Ellie had told him about the retail store, but he hadn't expected the parking lot to be so crowded. But it was Saturday afternoon, and tourists and locals alike would want to enjoy the summer sunshine.

Travis bypassed the impressive new store and headed for the marina's office. Striding along the dock, he automatically took in the changes. Sandy and Ellie had added two new fuel pumps and several rows of slips. They'd purchased a new forklift, and one of the operators was in the process of moving a boat from dry storage to the water.

On a busy Saturday, Ellie was usually tuning up one of the boat engines. He and his sister shared an aptitude for all things mechanical, and he kept searching for her to pop up from an engine compartment, a smudge of grease on her cheek. But when he didn't see Ellie anywhere, disappointment and worry slashed him. She wasn't in the bait house, or directing traffic at the ramp, or at the tool shed.

Travis headed directly to the office. The old mahogany door sported new gold-leaf lettering that read Vale & Cantrel Enterprises, with operating hours posted right next to a plastic sign that said Closed. Travis knocked anyway. The girls often used the Closed sign instead of Do Not Disturb, which everyone ignored. Besides, he could see Sandy through the glass, her head bent as she perused assorted paperwork.

Sandy's waist-length tresses were gone. Now, bright yellow sunglasses, worn above her forehead, held her shoulder-length blond locks out of her eyes, giving him a clear view of her face. Sandy wasn't model pretty. Her mouth was a bit too full and her nose had a cute little bump where she'd broken it windsailing. Her flawless skin was sun-kissed and far too tan. Nevertheless, Sandy was the only woman he'd ever met who sizzled. She had this unexplainable electric energy to her that never failed to engage his senses—at full throttle. Long ago, the passion between them had been charged, but their arguments had been long, horrendous and ugly. Once, she'd been like a fancy-free flame that attracted him with her heat and brightness, but when he'd gotten too close, she hadn't just scorched him, she'd burned him to the bone.

Nothing short of fear for Ellie could have brought him back. Bracing for bad news, stiffening his defenses against Sandy's magnificent eyes—they changed color like the sea, from sparkling turquoise when she was happy, to kelp-green when her temper raged, he strode into the office.

A sixth sense must have told her he was at the door, because he'd no more than turned the knob before she'd shot out of her seat behind the desk and rushed to him, flung her arms around his neck and planted a kiss on his mouth. A kiss that sent his senses spinning. A kiss that made the intervening years disappear with magic. A kiss that overloaded his pleasure centers and stole his breath.

Whoa. After eight years, this was not the reunion he'd imagined. No how. No way. Sandy might be one laid-back woman, but she could bear a grudge for a long time. After their last fight, he expected her to hold his words against him forever.

She tasted of salt and sea air and a citrus fragrance that reminded him of spiced lemons. And she fit against him just the way he remembered. Automatically, he raised his arms around her. Their tongues tangled, and in another moment she was going to find out that she still made all the blood in his brain flow south. But she pulled back, her eyes a tempestuous green, and placed a finger over his lips.

What the hell? She hadn't spoken to him in years, then left a worrisome message on his voice mail, and now she didn't want him to speak. Every brain cell cried out for him to ask about Ellie, but, as if reading his mind, Sandy shook her head.

"You still good with engines, Travis?"

Confused, his eyes narrowed. Sandy didn't play games. She hadn't placed a worried-crazy message on his voice mail without good reason. And from the tension in her shoulders to the tight grip of her hand on his arm, he knew something was wrong.

"You called me—"

"To fix a motor. Didn't you say you needed a job?" Her eyes begged him to play along.

Job? They hadn't even spoken. What the hell was going on here?

He shrugged to release the tension between his shoulder blades. "Yeah. I'm at loose ends right now. I could use some work, but I didn't bring my tools."

Relief warmed the chill from her eyes. She grabbed a sweater from a hook by the door. "Tools I can lend you. Can you start today?"

"Do I get time and a half?"

"That depends how good you are."

"You know how good I am," he bantered playfully, but if she didn't explain soon, his teeth might crack from the way he was gnashing them. Accustomed to cloak-and-dagger stuff at work, Travis hadn't expected to return home to a mystery.

Years ago, when he'd been responsible for Ellie, he'd been in a relationship with Sandy. Many of their arguments had been over Ellie. Sandy had considered him too restrictive and over-the-top protective. She'd once told him that if he could have, he'd never have let Ellie out of the house, never mind on a date. But Ellie had enjoyed pushing him to the wall, dating bikers, surfers and all-around misfits. At first he'd been pleased when Sandy had taken Ellie under her wing, but then he'd realized Sandy had been encouraging his sister's rebelliousness. After numerous heated arguments, he and Sandy had split up—but the girls had become fast friends.

Travis had been none too pleased when Ellie and Sandy joined forces in business. He didn't like the idea of his sister gallivanting all over the ocean with only one other woman. They were vulnerable, and obviously something bad had happened or Sandy wouldn't have called him.

"Come on." Sandy led him through the office door onto the dock. "I'm in critical need of a top-notch mechanic."

"What—"

"Give me a second." She squeezed his hand so tight, the bones creaked. "The boat's over here. The motor's on the fritz."

"You want to clarify?"

Sandy tugged the sunglasses from her forehead down over her eyes. "She's overheating when kept below two knots. The owner has out-of-town guests and is impatient to take her out tomorrow." Travis didn't give a damn. He wanted to know about Ellie. But he held his tongue, grabbed a toolbox from the shed and acted as if he intended to fix the motor as Sandy led him to a day-sailer with an outboard on its transom.

He half expected Sandy to tell him that Ellie had hooked up with some guy with a record. Or some loner who lived on a houseboat, collected disability checks and drank away his benefits. Ellie had always had a soft spot for those who were down and out. And she never thought of the danger she might be placing herself in. Every time Travis had tried to talk with her, she'd told him off.

So he'd taught her to fight dirty. But she'd refused to learn to shoot a weapon or keep one aboard. Sandy hadn't been any more reasonable. Both of them seemed to believe that they were impervious to trouble. But Travis had always known that two women alone at sea were targets. It was amazing they'd gotten along just fine on their own—although he had no doubts that Ellie filtered what she told him about her adventures. There was no telling how many close calls they'd had, how many scrapes they'd been in that he didn't know about.

Since the two women listened to nothing he said, perhaps his ignorance was bliss. It had certainly been less stressful—until now.

Travis stepped aboard and headed for the engine. He checked the fuel first. The tank was full. He yanked the power cord once and wasn't all that surprised when the motor fired right up. There was no extra smoke, no sign of the overheating she'd mentioned. In fact, the only thing close to overheating was his temper.

Travis didn't want to tell Sandy, "I told you so." He wanted to know that his sister was safe, that Sandy had brought him here for no reason other than to irritate him. But the knot in his gut told him otherwise. So did the tension in Sandy's jaw, where a muscle ticked. He'd never seen her wound so tight.

With her laid-back attitude, Sandy usually looked at life through mellow-toned glasses. But her live-and-let-live philosophy seemed to apply to everyone but Travis. According to Sandy, years ago, he could do nothing right. He knew nothing about women, nothing about teenage girls and nothing about parenting.

What made their fights so tempestuous was that Sandy had been partially right. But what twenty-two-year-old dude was ready to take on raising a rebellious teenage sister and have a serious relationship? Travis had done his best. And he couldn't have screwed up too badly with Ellie because she had turned out just fine. She didn't do drugs. She didn't drink too much. And she had good friends. If she went too easily from one man to the next, Travis didn't see what he could do about it. Ellie was a grown woman, but obviously she'd tangled with something bad enough for Sandy to break her silent treatment of Travis and call him.

He wanted an explanation, but Sandy left him to man the tiller while she cast off the lines. Amid gulls squawking, and other boaters waving as they passed by, they cruised out of the protected harbor. Travis kept one eye on the temperature gauge and saw no sign of a malfunction.

Sandy returned to the cockpit and sat next to him, crossing her long, tanned legs. "Sorry for the dramatics. I'm pretty sure that my office and phones are bugged."

Travis frowned, pulled the tiller to his body and motored around a channel marker. "Where's Ellie?"

"Our last client kidnapped her."

“What?” Travis didn’t hold back several four-letter words. His temper, already on a short fuse, lit up. It worried him that Sandy didn’t even bother to shout back—a sure sign of serious trouble.

“At least pretend to fiddle with the engine, and I’ll tell you everything.” While he removed the engine’s hood, Sandy’s eyes brimmed with tears and she wiped them off her cheeks. He’d never seen her cry, and his gut churned with fear. “We’d been paid by Danzler to deliver a boat to a private island off Nova Scotia owned by a Martin Vanderpelt. When we got there, Vanderpelt examined the boat, discovered it wasn’t the exact one he’d ordered and went ballistic.”

“I don’t understand.”

“His boat had been struck by lightning. Danzler had a duplicate hull on hand and filled his order. But Vanderpelt insisted we return for the original damaged hull and made us take his associate, Alan Lavelle, with us.”

“You took on a passenger?”

“He pulled a gun on us.”

“Go on.” Travis forced himself to appear outwardly calm, but inside he tensed up with fear for Ellie. Taking out a wrench from the toolbox, he pretended to use it, his concerns for Ellie escalating with every word Sandy spoke. The defeat lacing her words scared him as much as her story.

“So the three of us sailed back to Danzler Marine only to learn Vanderpelt’s original boat had been stolen. We decided to return home to wait for Danzler, the insurance company and the police to find the boat, or decide what to do next. That's when Alan grabbed Ellie and forced her into a motorboat that came alongside us. He told me that when I found Vanderpelt's boat and brought it to the island, he'd release Ellie."

"Why didn't you call the cops?"

"He said I'd be watched. And that if I went to the authorities, Ellie would suffer consequences." Sandy met his eyes, her own still teary. "I called you from a pay phone, but was afraid to answer your calls. They are watching me. I don't know who or where or how, but I've heard clicks on my phone, and there are people hanging around the marina that I've never seen before."

Travis forced himself into professional mode. He couldn't allow his fears to overwhelm him if he was going to help his sister. "When did they take Ellie?"

"Yesterday afternoon."

"What kind of boat was it?"

"A Grady-White with double Mercury engines. The first five numbers of the serial are 47583."

"You did good." He tossed the wrench back into the toolbox. "What can you tell me about Alan Lavelle?"

"Not much. He was medium height, medium build. Nondescript. He didn't talk much, and said nothing about himself or Vanderpelt. He didn't seem to know boats, but the closer we got to land, the edgier he became."

"You think he took Ellie back to Vanderpelt's island?"

"I don't know." Sandy's voice cracked. "He could have taken her anywhere."

"What did Danzler Marine say about the missing boat?"

"They filed a police report and are collecting a claim from their insurance company." She shrugged. "They'll probably be happier if the boat's never found. Lightning weakened the hull, and that's not easy to fix."

He saw regret in her eyes, and something more. "What else?"

"Alan called me this morning. He told me I had to deliver the boat alone. But I protested, telling him I couldn't handle it by myself and needed a mechanic. So he okayed one crew member."

"That was good thinking." Sandy had done remarkably well under trying circumstances. This kind of pressure often caused people to fall apart, and they failed to think clearly. He made his voice warm, despite the chill in his heart. "I'm glad you called me."

"I didn't have much choice." She lifted her chin and squared her shoulders as if bracing for a blow. He didn't understand why. They might have fought like dogs over a scrap of meat, but they'd never come to blows. Although during some of their past fights, Sandy had made him angry enough to lose his temper, Travis had never lashed out with violence. But she was steeling herself as if she expected him to go postal.

"What?" he asked.

"Alan said if we didn't bring him the boat within ten days, he'd…" She swallowed hard.

"He'd what?"

"He'd kill Ellie."

ELLIE WAS ALTERNATELY terrified, angry and restless. When Alan had forced her from the sailboat, she'd been shaking so hard, she'd barely understood that she was being kidnapped, never mind comprehended all the ramifications.

Right now, pessimism had her hugging her knees and wondering how anyone would find her. The ride in the Grady-White had been short. Once they'd raced out of sight of Sandy, they'd switched to a sturdy cabin cruiser, and Alan had locked Ellie in the forward cabin. She had a bunk, a head and a shower. The portholes didn't open. He'd locked the hatch from outside. Not even Houdini could have escaped. And even if she smashed open the door—a feat that would take considerable force—she would have to face two armed men, Alan and his cohort.

Twice a day, Alan brought her food. The rest of the time, she was alone in the cabin with her thoughts. She tried, and failed, not to think about Alan's threat to kill her. She tried not to think about how easily they could shoot her, toss her body overboard, and no one would ever know what had happened to her.

Instead, she attempted to think of a reason for her predicament. Why did Vanderpelt want that original boat so much? A boat with a damaged hull? Nothing made sense. Either he was insane or she was missing too many facts. She hadn't a clue why he'd gone to such extremes to retrieve a damaged sailboat.

She still couldn't believe their bad luck that Vanderpelt's boat had been stolen. And she had no idea how Sandy would find it. Yet, she had every confidence in her best friend and partner. For Ellie's sake, Sandy would overcome her disinclination to contact Travis. And the Shey Group, the powerful and secret organization of which her brother was a vital part, would hunt down Vanderpelt and rescue her. At least, that's what Ellie told herself in her optimistic moments.

Ellie slept as much as she could over the next four days. Still, with no one to talk to and nothing to read, the time passed slowly. Contradictorily, she dreaded the end of the voyage.

But late on the fourth day of her captivity, Alan unlocked her cabin door. He tossed a black hood to her. "Put that on."

His face was cold, his dark eyes, almost dead, like a zombie in those creepy horror movies. And his voice, so lacking in intonation, sent icy stabs of pain into her chest.

There was no point in fighting him. Not when just beyond him, in the main cabin, the other man waited. Mouth dry with fear, Ellie told herself they hadn't brought her all this way to shoot her. With trembling fingers, she placed the hood over her head.

"Stand up and turn around."

She forced her rubbery knees to support her. Willed herself not to fight, despite the hood that not only blinded but suffocated.

"Cross your wrists behind your back."

Oh...God. She hesitated, and Alan roughly grabbed her hands and bound her wrists with tough, rigid plastic. As if all the moisture had been sucked out of her mouth, she couldn't swallow. "What—"

"Silence." Alan slapped her cheek and she stumbled, her shoulder slamming into the bulkhead.

Her ears ringing, her nose clogging, her eyes filling with tears, Ellie reeled from the stinging blow to her cheek. But the pain was nothing compared to the terror bleeding through her veins. Unwilling to provoke her captor again, Ellie remained silent. Although Travis had taught her to fight, there was no point in revealing her skills and giving up the advantage of surprise until she stood a real chance of escape.

The deck squeaked, giving her warning that Alan approached again, and despite herself, she cringed. He didn't strike her, but his hand roughly clasped her upper arm and jerked her to her feet. Then shoved her through the main cabin and outside. She walked a gangplank to a floating dock that rose and fell with the wave action.

Listening carefully for clues as to her whereabouts, she heard seagulls' caws and the whipping wind rustling leaves. There were no sounds of halyards clanging against masts, or the creak of boats at anchorage. Wherever they'd taken her, it wasn't a marina. And since they led her about openly with the hood on her head, she could only conclude they weren't worried about someone spotting her and reporting her predicament to the authorities.

Was she back on Vanderpelt's island?

The time spent at sea was about right to have made the return. But she had no way of knowing if they'd come due north, south or east or any combination between. Tilting her head downward, she spied slivers of green grass and gravel by her feet. And what little air passed through her hood smelled of the sea.

Ellie had no idea how long they walked in silence, but she counted her steps. Two thousand and ten. Alan jerked her to a stop, and she heard the clink of a key inserting into, then turning, a lock. Alan spun her around, removed the plastic from her wrists, then shoved her forward.

Ellie barely got her hands in front of her in time to break her fall onto what felt like a mattress. The door slammed behind her and the lock slid home. Yanking the hood from her head, she blinked in the dim, gray light, finding herself in a new prison. The walls were stones set in cement, the tiny, high windows revealed only sky. The door was solid metal. Inside her four walls, she had a mattress on the floor, a toilet and sink in the far corner. No shower. No light. No tools.

On hands and knees Ellie examined the walls, but the solid stone gave her no hope of escape. She stood on the toilet, but still could see nothing but sky outside. And the sink's plumbing fittings were solid, nothing she could loosen with just her bare hands. Ellie wanted to lie on the bed and cry herself to sleep. She didn't. Instead, she lifted the mattress until it rested flush with one wall. The floor beneath the mattress was stone, like the walls. She couldn't dig her way out.

Now what?

She needed to think. And nothing got the blood pumping and the mind working like a little exercise.

Ellie warmed up with slow stretches, then ran in place until her breath came in gasps. After slowly walking in place to cool down her heart rate a little, she did push-ups. Isometrics. And then a final series of stretches.

And didn't feel one damn bit better. She was still a prisoner without any hope of escape.

Ellie drank cold water from the sink, then kicked the mattress back onto the floor. She was about to lie down when the voices of two men drifted to her. Hurrying to the wall, she pressed her ear against the stone.

A man spoke gruffly. "You don't look happy."

"I've never killed a woman," another man said, his tone somber.

"Hey, man. It's just like running your blade through a tough piece of steak."

The peace Ellie had won for herself through her exercise disintegrated. Stumbling away from the wall, she'd barely flopped onto the mattress before the door opened and one of the men shoved a bowl of food in her direction. When she didn't get up fast enough to take it, he dropped the bowl. The ceramic dish broke, and her soup splashed on the floor, walls and mattress.

Chuckling, he slammed and relocked the door.

Ellie hadn't been hungry. But at the sight of the spilled soup, she burst into tears.

"Come get me, Sandy," she sobbed, lying on her side, her knees pulled to her chest. "Travis, please find me. Soon."

Chapter Two

Sandy waited for Travis to shout at her. To tell her how irresponsible she'd been. That Ellie's life was in danger because she'd led his little sister into a dangerous situation. She braced for him to yell at her for refusing to keep weapons on board, for accepting a commission from a stranger. But without saying one word, Travis flipped open his cell phone.

Arrogant as ever, Travis hadn't listened to her warning that if they contacted the authorities, Ellie would be killed. Sandy didn't wait for him to press the send button, she grabbed for the phone. "Don't!"

Travis pulled the phone away. He'd always had the most amazing reflexes, but she'd forgotten exactly how fast he could move. She'd also forgotten how he could drill her with one of his I-know-better-than-you-do looks that always made her furious. Anger at him chased back some of her fear. Until she looked, really looked, at Travis's face, and realized he was more dangerous now.

He'd changed during the last eight years. The gaunt lines of youth had been replaced by the solid maturity of a man. If possible, he'd grown more handsome, more cocky. His shoulders had broadened, his chest had thickened with powerful muscles that tapered to a flat stomach. But his face, with its bold nose and square jaw, remained compelling. His dark hair that gleamed in the sunlight was still thick, but cut short. She didn't understand how his eyes, the exact same smoky gray as Ellie's, could convey such harsh disapproval with just a glance. "My phone call will bounce through four continents and five satellites. The message is encrypted with a code not even the Pentagon can break. You needn't fear anyone will listen in."

The Travis she'd known wouldn't have explained at all, but this Travis gave her the opportunity to offer an opinion. "Yeah, but when they can't break your code, do you suppose they'll think you're one of the authorities they told me not to contact?"

Sandy didn't know why she bothered to argue. Travis never listened to her. Now that he was thirty, and undoubtedly more set in his ways, she was probably wasting her breath. The hard look on his face, the grim set of his mouth, warned her to choose her words carefully. For Ellie's sake, she had to work with him. If she'd had any other choice, she'd never have called Travis. But with

Ellie's life on the line, she'd do anything to help her—even put up with her brother again. While Sandy didn't know exactly what Travis did for a living, she knew it was high-tech, dangerous and clandestine work for a secret organization that worked with the U.S. government.

Sandy had expected Travis to come charging in to save Ellie. She'd known he'd be full of himself, but she needed his expertise. So when, after considering her words, he pressed the off button and said, "Good point," her jaw dropped.

The Travis she'd known would never have admitted that she had a good idea, never mind let her suggestion change his mind. Perhaps along with his body's maturing, his mind had grown wiser. Or perhaps his fear for Ellie was making him consider other options. Whatever accounted for the change in him, she hoped he'd learned to control the temper that fueled him.

If Travis's temper had been a motor, it would have run on high octane. If his temper had been a boat, it would have been a sleek racer, raring to go and easily tipped. And if his temper had been a storm, it would have been a nor'easter—powerful, raging and disastrous.

Years ago, Sandy had decided she didn't want to drown in one of his storms. And yet, she'd always been drawn to the passion that drove him. There was a turbulence to Travis that made him the most exciting man she'd ever known, but that attraction came with a cost—a price so high, that being around him was dangerous to her well-being.

After the most passionate of flings, Sandy had concluded she couldn't live in the chaos that always surrounded Travis. Their breakup had been painful, but necessary. She'd cut her losses and gone on. And as a means of self-protection, she'd avoided Travis during his infrequent trips to visit Ellie. For her own sanity, she didn't want to risk falling for him again. Incredible passion wasn't worth the accompanying heartache.

"We need help. I'll wait until I can use a land line and a pay phone."

She couldn't believe her ears. Travis, the original Mr. Go-It-Alone, had become a team player. Stunned by his transformation, Sandy realized that the man she was sitting beside must have gone through more than she'd imagined to have changed so much. Ellie had hinted that Travis's stint in the Special Forces had taken a toll, but Sandy hadn't wanted to discuss him—not when the subject was so raw and painful. So Ellie had honored her wishes and rarely mentioned his name.

She peered at Travis over her sunglasses. "I'm all for getting help, but if there's any chance of a leak…"

His eyes snapped with the old temper, but he kept it caged. "We need help with Vanderpelt. The Shey Group, the people I work with, will get me Vanderpelt's history—everything from where he was born to where he keeps his money. I need to know who Vanderpelt trusts. Where he's from. What other property he owns. Everything about his business, to make the right decisions."

"You have access to that kind of information?"

He nodded. "We also need blueprints of the island.

Satellite photos might tell us if Ellie is there. We may need an assault team to land. Or a secret approach might be better, depending on the number of men and defensive positions. I need expert military analysis. We don't have the time, expertise or equipment to do this all alone."

Travis sounded as if he knew what he needed, as if he was an expert. And a stranger. Instead of responding emotionally, he'd laid out a plan in a logical progression that had clued her into the fact that the organization he worked for must have extraordinary resources. "Okay. But Vanderpelt expects you and me to deliver his boat. We've got to find it, repair it, then sail it to his island."

"The Shey Group can help us there, too."

Travis spoke as if he had no doubt his organization would help them. She didn't question his judgment, because one thing hadn't changed—Travis had always loved his sister. And Sandy had no doubt he would do whatever it took to rescue her. Making the decision to call Travis had been difficult. She'd worried that his hotheaded temper would hurt her chance of rescuing Ellie, but now she was very glad to have Travis at her side.

Sandy knew that boats often disappeared and were never seen again. It was too easy for a professional thief to steal a boat in the middle of the night, change the serial numbers and sail off to another country to sell it. The Coast Guard couldn't cover every cove and harbor along the U.S. border. And marinas simply operated on too small a profit margin to employ night watchmen. Usually, the insurance company paid off the claim and the owner purchased a new boat. Finding Vanderpelt's missing vessel was not going to be easy.

"How can the Shey Group help with the boat?"

"We have contacts in the Coast Guard, the navy and the police. If Vanderpelt's boat shows up on any official radar, we'll know about it."

Travis's certainty gave her a measure of relief. "You're assuming Alan and his associate didn't sink her, or change the serial number."

"I'm not assuming anything. Can you put out word to the local sailors, and at the marina, that we need to find that boat? Also, if we can get a line on the Grady-White, it might give us a clue as to who we're dealing with."

She nodded. "The grapevine is as good as ever." Fishermen, local guides and pleasure boaters were a tight community. When one of their own needed help, everyone pitched in.

Travis turned the boat around, heading back to the marina. "I'll order us some jamming equipment. We have to be able to communicate without fear of someone listening."

Travis sounded sure of his technical expertise, but she still feared his equipment could give away their plans. "But, if we jam the signal, won't they become suspicious?"

"Not necessarily. Let me deal with it."

Were they actually working together? It was difficult to believe that she and Travis had had a conversation without ending up in bed or shouting at one another. This had to be a first. And she hoped it would continue.

After they returned to the marina, Sandy typed up a description of Vanderpelt's boat. She offered a reward for any information, then used the copy machine to make flyers. Her assistant manager would post some at the marina. But she took the majority of the flyers, and a stapler, with her. She and Travis drove up and down the coast, stopping in marinas, bait shops and boat dealers to put them up and talk to people about the missing boat. At this time of year, the waterways were crowded with boaters on summer vacation. Everyone promised to keep their eyes peeled during their journeys.

While Sandy worked, Travis stopped at local bars. He used the pay phones repeatedly, never staying on the line for more than thirty seconds. Then they'd both return to her vehicle and head to the next spot.

Travis checked the sideview mirror for what must have been the hundredth time. "I wish I could pick up a tail."

"Why?" She was driving since Travis was barhopping. In case anyone was watching, he'd ordered a beer every place he'd stopped. But he probably hadn't drunk much, because he still appeared clearheaded. Even in their younger days, Travis might have been a hell-raiser, but he hadn't been much of a drinker. He liked fast cars and faster boats, but he always said high speeds and drinking didn't mix.

"A tail might give us some clues. Vanderpelt is like chasing a ghost."

She didn't like the frustration in Travis's tone, or the discouragement in the set of his shoulders. "What do you mean, he's a ghost?"

"Vanderpelt is not a U.S. or Canadian citizen. His name is probably an alias. A corporation owns the island, but it's a subsidiary of a Swiss company. Normally, the Swiss are not into sharing their financial information with us. But since 9/11, and thanks to a favor Logan Kincaid did for their embassy people in Saudi Arabia, they told us the Swiss company is part of a Libyan conglomerate, headquartered in Tripoli."

"So you don't know who he is or where he's from?"

"Yeah."

"If his business is that extensive, surely someone must—"

"His cover is deep. We are not dealing with a common criminal. With his connections and wealth, he's likely tied to any one of a dozen criminal organizations, the Russian Mafia, the Colombian cartels, the Chinese, the Bulgarians—take your pick."

"So rescuing Ellie is going to be—"

"We'll get her. These people won't kill her as long as she's of use to them. We have ten days, and we're going to make use of every hour, every second."

The determination in his tone bucked up her flagging hopes. Travis knew better than Sandy what they were up against. If he thought they could find and rescue Ellie, then it had to be possible. And meanwhile, Sandy would do her best to put her survivor's guilt away. She'd never understood why Alan had taken Ellie as hostage and not her, except that she couldn't get out of her mind the way Vanderpelt had leered at the sight of Ellie's legs. Sandy said nothing to Travis about that look. He had enough worries, and he was already doing everything he could think of to find Ellie. But she also felt guilty that she hadn't stepped forward and suggested Alan take her in place of Ellie. Taking the Vanderpelt commission had been Sandy's idea. She was the older partner, and it should have been her taken hostage. But Alan had grabbed Ellie without warning, and Sandy had been so stunned, she simply hadn't thought fast enough to do more than protest.

Driving up and down the coast stapling flyers to telephone poles didn't seem like enough. Sandy wanted to do more. She wanted some hint that Ellie was still alive. The minutes seemed to tick by like months, and the stress kept her stomach churning.

If she didn't known Travis better, she might have thought he had his emotions under total control. But every once in a while, their gazes crossed and she glimpsed desperation and bleak despair, along with fierce determination. They ate a late dinner of clam chowder and burgers. She barely tasted her food, but her body needed the fuel.

When they exited the restaurant, it was dark. Most day boaters would have come in and trailered their boats home hours ago. Those spending the night on the water would be anchored in a safe harbor, or tucked into a slip for the night. For her part, Sandy could do nothing more. But Travis had a restless energy that told her he wasn't ready to quit.

She was about to suggest heading back to her marina when Travis's cell phone beeped. He checked the caller ID. "I need to use the pay phone."

For the first time that day, she accompanied him while he made a call. She was surprised how long it took to go through, but then, he'd dialed an international number. She was praying Ellie had escaped, and someone was calling Travis to let them know his sister was okay. But she knew how unlikely that was. Despite her impatience, Sandy refrained from asking questions Travis couldn't answer.

"Travis, here." He spoke into the phone, his voice deep and confident.

Shifting from one foot to the other, she fidgeted and looked for clues on Travis's face whether the news was good or bad. His eyes narrowed, but he nodded as he listened, and she had the impression some progress had been made.

"Thanks. We can be there in an hour."

"Where?"

"Pine Key. Some windsailers found the Grady-White on a sand bar. She washed in with the tide. We're meeting the Coast Guard and a forensic team there."

Forensic team? Her knees buckled and Sandy clutched Travis's arm. "Oh, God. Are there bodies?"

TRAVIS CURSED HIMSELF as he stared down at Sandy's pale face and quivering lower lip. "No bodies. The forensic team will comb the boat for clues to who stole the boat then sank her."

"Ellie?" Sandy still clutched him, but her death grip had lightened somewhat.

"We don't know where she is." Right now that was

good news to Sandy, who'd believed that Ellie's body might have been on the sunken boat. Travis had no excuse for scaring her. His mind had been on Kincaid's news, and he'd stupidly frightened Sandy when he knew better. She'd been on edge all day. Exhaustion darkened her eyes and guilt stabbed him. She was worried out of her mind, and his carelessness could have sent her over the edge into hysteria. "I'm sorry for scaring you."

Travis took Sandy into his arms, and it seemed the most natural move in the world. She needed solid reassurance. He had to insure she wouldn't go to pieces on him. However, as her fresh scent—a pine shampoo she favored—drifted into his system with the potency of bubbling wine, he ached to hold her for longer than was necessary. When the smooth texture of her cheek brushed his jaw, it took all his self-control not to slant his lips over hers. Like a powerful high tide rushing in during a full moon, his elemental reaction to her almost swept him under. He simply wasn't prepared to want her—not with all the years that had passed. Not with all the bad memories. Not with Ellie out there somewhere, waiting for them to rescue her. Stunned how Sandy affected him, Travis refrained from dipping his head to sip a taste of her mouth.

Already her color was returning, and her lower lip ceased quivering. "I should slap you upside the head for scaring me like that."

She didn't mean it. The tough talk was to cover up her momentary panic. He squeezed her tightly, then released her and stepped back. "If hitting me will make you feel better, go ahead."

"Naw. I'd only hurt my hand on that stubborn jaw of yours." She straightened. "But if you ever do that to me again, I swear I'll deck you."

"And I'd deserve it." Not that she could hurt him. His reflexes had been honed from years of hand-to-hand practice in a half dozen martial arts. Travis held out his hand for the keys. "You're tired. Why don't you let me drive?"

She'd always claimed that he drove too fast to be trusted with her vehicle, but she handed over the keys with only minor hesitation. The truth was, he did drive too fast. But he had great reflexes. And he knew this road as well as he knew the expressions on Sandy's face. He'd spent his youth driving up and down this coast, and could anticipate every curve, every light, fork and town. And he damn well wouldn't risk an accident when Ellie's life hung in the balance.

He kept his speed down to five miles over the limit, but it seemed to take forever before they reached Pine Key. Once a one-lane, covered wooden bridge for horse-drawn carriages, the bridge had been renovated several times over the past century. Now, two lanes of concrete, asphalt and steel, the bridge was high enough for smaller boats to pass under. The island beyond, with its protected cove, was a favorite anchorage for pleasure craft. Tonight, a police helicopter, several Coast Guard patrol boats and a barge with a crane disrupted the darkness and peace of the isolated spot.

Travis crossed the short bridge and parked. As he and Sandy exited, the crane roared to life and pulled a boat from the water. Lights from the surrounding craft and automobiles focused on the hull, and four holes in the bottom could clearly be seen where water spouted out.

"Those holes are perfectly round," Sandy muttered. "They sank her on purpose."

After Travis identified himself to a cop, he and Sandy strode up a long gangplank and boarded the barge where the crane operator gently lowered the damaged boat to the deck. A team of gloved forensic people immediately went to work, crawling through the hull in search of evidence. Since the boat had been underwater for hours, the sea would likely have washed away microscopic clues. But maybe they'd luck out and find a jacket lodged in a seat back, keys or identification coated in plastic.

Several people on shore watched the proceedings, and Travis wondered if any were taking undue notice of his and Sandy's actions. Several times today, he'd thought someone might be following them. But despite his vigilance, he'd never spotted the same stranger twice. Which meant either he was suffering from paranoia, or the people watching them were switching off, indicating a coordinated effort and professional action that required substantial economic means.

Travis and Sandy joined the investigators, who'd carefully set an anchor and line inside a clear plastic bag. In other bags, Travis spied several life jackets, a flare, a screwdriver and an extra portable gas tank. No one bothered dusting for prints. Each item would be examined for DNA evidence, but it was unlikely blood, hair, or even a fingernail would have survived the assault of the sea.

The lead investigator, a pudgy, pleasant-face man with piercing eyes, joined Travis and Sandy as if he'd been expecting them. "I'm chief investigator George Foster."

"Travis Cantrel and Sandy Vale." Travis, then Sandy, shook George's hand.

The amenities done, George went right to business. "The plastic serial numbers on the hull were removed before they sank her, but we lucked out. Whoever scraped off the plastic was in a hurry. We've matched the serial numbers to the ones Sandy remembered, so we don't have to wait on a match from the engine's manufacturer. This is definitely your boat. Logan Kincaid said that you'd want to contact the owner yourself." George slipped a piece of paper into Travis's hand. "I'll give you a thirty-minute head start before I turn that information over to the local cops."

"Thanks." Travis tried to control his impatience. While there was a chance the owner of this boat knew where Ellie was, they might have difficulty finding him. Still, they might drive to the boat owner's house, luck out and find both him and Ellie there.

George Foster seemed to understand Travis's immediate need to track down their next lead. "Go. Your boss, Kincaid, is a good man. My number's on that paper, too. Anything else I can do, let me know."

"Appreciate it." Travis nodded. "If you find more on the boat—"

"You'll be the first to know. Kincaid gave me your cell number. But don't expect us to find much. She's been submerged almost twenty-four hours."

"I understand." Travis took Sandy's hand and they hurried toward the car. He slipped into the driver's seat, fastened his seat belt and handed her the address. "Which way?"

"Let me check the map." She reached into the glove compartment and turned on an interior light. Although every nerve in him screamed to drive fast, until he had a direction, he restrained his impatience.

Sandy had a great sense of direction. If he gave her a moment to orient herself, she'd find the fastest route. Gazing down at the map, her lips pursed in concentration and she focused intently. He recalled that, despite all her laid-back ways, she usually got the job done, working at her own pace.

Turning the marina into a profitable enterprise had taken both hard work and good business sense. It also fit Sandy's need for freedom. A nonconformist, she liked to set her own hours and wear whatever fashion struck her. She rarely slept in past dawn. However, she needed her afternoon nap, and often turned cranky late at night.

He'd bet she hadn't slept since Ellie's disappearance and, with the hour close to midnight, she had to be ready to drop. Yet, she hadn't complained once about her exhaustion. After she gave him the directions, he tuned the radio to a local easy-listening station. Elevator music, as she called it. Music that would put her to sleep.

"Why don't you close your eyes," he suggested.

"You'll wake me when we arrive?"

"Yeah."

Sandy bunched her sweater against the door to pillow her head, but despite his effort to drive smoothly, she couldn't relax. After fifteen minutes, she opened her eyes and flicked the radio to hard rock. The sounds of Jimi Hendrix filled the car, bringing back memories of loud beach parties, roasting marshmallows over an open fire, skinny-dipping and lusty sex. The one good thing about all of Sandy and Travis's fights had been when they made up, the sex was always fantastic.

"Travis?" Sandy's voice was low and throaty.

"Yeah?"

"You think there's any chance Ellie could be with the boat's owner?"

"It's possible—but unlikely. Before we knock on the door, I need to stop and use the pay phone. By now, I'm hoping we have some background intel on the boat's owner, Kevin Baine."

Travis would have preferred to use his cell phone. But headlights in his rearview mirror kept him antsy. The car never drew close enough for him to see a driver. And when he pulled over, the vehicle kept going. But Travis knew a good tail wouldn't blow his cover by stopping. Instead, he'd hide up ahead, turn off his lights and—once they'd passed by—jump back on their tail.

He pulled off the road at a convenience store, dialed the pay phone and waited for the connection. "It's Travis."

Ryker Stevens, a friend of Travis, and Kincaid's best intel specialist, took the call. "Kevin Baine. U.S. citizen. He's an army veteran. Honorably discharged. He makes his living driving a truck. No arrests. No suspicious activity. He looks clean, but I'll keep digging."

"Thanks."

Travis got back into the car. For three miles, the road behind him remained empty. They had passed no rest stops or crossroads. And then headlights appeared behind them again, as if someone had been waiting for them.

Chapter Three

"What's wrong?" Sandy asked, as Travis hit town and peeled right through a yellow light.

"Someone's tailing us. I want to lose him before we meet Kevin Baine."

At this time of night, there weren't many cars on the road. So Sandy's vehicle stood out like a sailboat trying to hide among a fleet of powerboats. When Travis pulled before a shopping center and doused the lights, she wasn't surprised. However, her pulse sped as she recalled Travis saying that he could pick up a lead if he could confront whoever was tailing them.

They waited for a tense ten minutes, but no one drove down the street. Sandy didn't know whether to be relieved or disappointed. On the one hand, they could use all the clues they could garner. On the other hand, she didn't like the idea of Travis confronting anyone.

Sandy told herself her concern for Travis was simply because she needed him to rescue Ellie. Between his skills and his connections, he had pull with government agencies that were actually cooperating. If she'd been on her own, those same people wouldn't have given her the time of day.

But the truth was also that she didn't want Travis hurt. Or worse. Intrigued by the man he'd become, she found that his sharp edges had developed into smooth curves that no longer sliced and diced. When she'd ended their relationship, she'd done so for her own peace of mind. Back then, she and Travis couldn't talk without going for one another's throats. So today, working and conversing with him without the discussion escalating into a top-of-the-lungs shouting match had been a pleasant surprise.

From the banked embers in his eyes to the tense clenching of his jaw, she could tell that Travis still had a hot temper. He still had blazing passion. But now he also had perspective that tempered his actions into systematic strategy.

She found herself asking his opinions and valuing his replies. "Do you think whoever was following us has given up?"

"We'll soon see." Travis started the engine, flipped on the headlights and drove around town. "If they are still looking for us, it'd be better to draw them out now, than have them surprise us after we reach Kevin Baine."

If the hour hadn't been so late, if most people in sleepy towns like this one hadn't been in bed well before midnight, Travis's scheme wouldn't have worked. They saw two delivery trucks, but no cars. After Travis trolled through town and no one took his bait, he steered for Kevin Baine's house.

The man lived up in the hills on a five-acre property covered with oak and pine trees. A white picket fence that had been freshly painted, and a pristine lawn, surrounded his two-story cottage perched on a hill. The covered front porch had a swing, the cushions sporting large yellow sunflowers. The rosebushes climbing the fence, the wind chimes and the bird feeder all suggested this was a well-loved home.

Travis had killed his lights when he'd turned down the road. He didn't pull into the driveway, but drove slowly past the premises. "There're burglar bars on the back window. And there's a night-light on in the kid's tree house."

She'd been looking at the rosebushes. He'd been trying to figure out if Ellie might be here. Exhaustion and stress must be getting to her, but she had difficulty believing that such a lovely setting could house the kind of evil that had taken Ellie from them.

A dog barked twice, then hushed. Travis parked the car up the street. Before opening the driver's door, he twisted the bulb so the interior lights wouldn't come on when he exited.

"If you want to come with me, you'll do exactly what I say." His tone wasn't arrogant or brash or superior. He used the tone of a man in charge of a mission, a man who knew what he was doing.

Once, she would have argued with him for assuming the leadership role. Now, she accepted that he was the expert, and agreed. “No problem.”

Perhaps Travis wasn’t the only one who had matured. She was now much more confident than she’d been all those years ago. She no longer needed to prove she could be independent. Not when she operated a successful business. Not when she was content with her life. She no longer had to challenge Travis at every turn and could accept that, when it came to tactics and dangerous situations, his training and special skills might be the difference between saving Ellie, and failure.

But she shouldn’t think about failure, not when she needed to keep her concentration on the present to help Travis and Ellie. Travis took Sandy’s hand and guided her along the shoulder of the road into the deep shadows. She appreciated the warmth of his flesh against hers, his quiet strength that infused her with courage.

Back in the car, she’d been certain Ellie couldn’t be here. That this house was the home of nice, normal people. But as the night air nipped at her flesh, and goose bumps rose from the chill, she not only wished she’d remembered to bring her sweater, but that she knew how to defend herself as well as Ellie did.

She’d always been so sure she could protect herself with common sense and words. But recent events had proven that she’d been seeing life through rose-colored glasses. Sandy might still have doubts about how well

Travis held his temper, but she never once doubted his ability to protect her. She didn't have to be an expert in combat to recognize how soundlessly he walked, how smoothly he blended into the darkness, how careful he could be.

He whispered into her ear. "Wait here. I'm going to check the windows."

For locks? To see inside? Before she asked, he was gone. And she felt vulnerable, exposed. She missed the warmth of his hand in hers as much as she missed his presence. She could only imagine what Ellie was feeling right now, all alone, with no idea if they would find her.

She'd been ripped from her life—and for what? So Vanderpelt could have his damn boat? Either the man was insane, or there was plenty they didn't know. Why was Vanderpelt so insistent on owning that particular hull? Had he stashed something in the keel? Drugs? Gold? What could be so important that he'd go to such extremes?

Sandy had no idea. A squirrel, or a chipmunk, raced across branches overhead, startling her. She peered through the darkness, searching for Travis's silhouette, but he'd disappeared like a breeze that kissed her cheek then melted away. He'd made his approach upwind of the house, so his scent wouldn't reach the dog they'd heard earlier, and she wondered if he was armed. If he intended to break into the house.

Waiting, not knowing his intentions, stretched her nerves tight.

All of a sudden, outside lights flooded the yard, catching Travis about twenty feet from the house. Either he'd set off motion detectors, or whoever was inside had spotted him. Heart pounding in her chest, she watched Travis drop to the ground and roll behind a car.

The front door opened and a man stayed in the shadows of the threshold, but pointed a shotgun at Travis. His voice deep and in control, the homeowner ordered, "Come out with your hands up. My wife is calling the police."

Oh…God.

No way could Travis crawl away without being shot. The floodlights had him pinned down. Sandy wanted to do something to help, but Travis had told her to stay where she was. If the homeowner was in league with the bad guys, no way would his wife be calling the police, as he'd just claimed. Sandy should stay hidden, then go straight to the police herself.

But if the homeowner was an innocent man who thought he was defending his property from a thief, Sandy might help Travis and Ellie if she came out of hiding.

Think.

Her mind raced. What should she do? Travis didn't want their presence here talked about openly over police channels. He'd told her it was too easy for the bad guys to pick up chatter on a scanner, and if anyone who was watching or listening found out that Sandy and Travis were doing more than trying to find Vanderpelt's boat, they might kill Ellie.

Sandy had a fraction of a second to make up her mind. A fraction of a second to decide whether to remain hidden in the shadows or to announce her presence to a man holding a shotgun. Yet, he hadn't fired at Travis. Maybe he didn't want to risk hitting his car, but he hadn't fired a warning shot, either. He was a veteran who knew how to handle a gun, and she made up her mind, praying he wouldn't shoot an unarmed woman without at least listening to her.

Raising her hands over her head, she stepped out of the darkness into the floodlights. "Please don't call the cops. A young woman's life is in danger."

"I told you to stay back." Travis practically growled from the shadows.

"And let you get shot? I don't think so. I need you to find Ellie. And besides, this gentleman has the wrong idea about you. He thinks you're a thief—not a man trying to find his kidnapped sister."

"Kidnapped sister?" Kevin Baine stepped beyond the threshold. In his early forties, his wavy, brown hair was starting to thin. Wrinkles around his eyes, and tanned skin, attested to a lifetime spent in the sun. A T-shirt and boxers suggested he'd been in bed before their sudden arrival. He didn't lower the shotgun, but clearly he was willing to listen.

Travis spoke softly, slowly edging out from behind the car, no weapon in sight. "Mr. Baine—"

"You know my name?"

Splitting Baine's attention between her and Travis—who also kept his hands up—Sandy spoke with urgency.

"We wanted to talk to you about your boat and my missing partner, his sister." She jerked her thumb in Travis's direction.

Baine kept the gun aimed at Travis. "So why didn't you knock on my door like honest folk?"

"My sister was kidnapped on your boat. I wanted to see if she was inside before I announced myself," Travis explained. "If your wife is really calling the police, could you delay that call—at least until you hear us out?" Travis requested, his manner polite. "Keep the gun on me—if you like. We need to talk."

Baine motioned with his gun for Travis to come forward. "If your sister was kidnapped, why don't you want the police—"

Sandy kept her hands high and walked right up to Baine. "Please. We mean you no harm. We were warned not to go to the cops or they'd kill Ellie."

Even as she approached Baine, the man kept his gun aimed at Travis. He wasn't distracted by her words, recognizing that the real threat was not her, but Travis. However, apparently, Baine had listened to her. He lifted the muzzle upward, and raised his voice so people inside could plainly hear him. "Darlene, cancel that call. We have us some visitors."

A woman peeked out of an upstairs window, waved, and then shouted down, "Don't stay out too late, dear."

Travis joined Sandy and put a tense arm over her shoulder. "You never listen to me."

"I listened. I just didn't comply."

"You could have gotten yourself shot."

"You were the one ducking behind the car," she pointed out.

Baine chuckled. "The lady's got a point. What's this about my stolen boat?"

Stolen? Damn. Vanderpelt was covering his tracks. A stolen boat couldn't lead back to him. And then, just to make sure, he'd sunk her to hide every clue.

"A couple of days ago, we were sailing." Sandy simplified her story. "Two men kidnapped Ellie—in your boat. We matched the serial numbers."

Baine set the shotgun butt on his front deck, but kept the weapon within easy reach. He appeared to be a reasonable man—but cautious. "My boat was stolen. The cops found the trailer, but the boat hasn't turned up."

"Actually, she has," Travis said. "The thieves drilled holes in the hull and sank her by Pine Key. Where did you keep the boat?"

"At a friend's dock. He had davits to lift her out, and that saved me the trouble of trailering her home every time someone answered my ad. My friend's on vacation in Europe. I agreed to watch his house in exchange for using his dock."

"Did anyone break into the house?" Travis asked.

Baine shook his head. "And they didn't touch his personal water vehicle, either."

"I'm assuming you reported the theft?"

"Of course. The police tried to dust the dock for prints but came up with zip."

"Thanks for your time, Mr. Baine. I'm sorry to have disturbed you." Travis reached out to shake the man's hand.

Baine shook it and volunteered, "You know, while the boat was up for sale, I had several visitors. Two days before she was stolen, some men came by to look at her. They checked her out stem to stern, and I thought they'd make an offer, but they never did. I told this to the cops, but they didn't seem too interested."

"What did the men look like?" Travis asked.

"White. Mid-thirties. I'm not too good with faces. One of them spoke with a thick accent."

Baine was trying to be helpful, but Sandy was too exhausted to comprehend how such general information could be of any use. Clearly, Vanderpelt had known that his own boat had been stolen before Ellie and she had arrived back in the States. So he'd made arrangements to have Ellie kidnapped to force Sandy to do his bidding. But why?

"What kind of accent?" Travis asked.

"If I had to guess, I'd say French."

"Travis." Sandy's excitement rose a notch. "The guy driving the boat that took Ellie spoke French. Just as they pulled away, I heard him say, '*Oui.*'"

"Anything else you can tell us about them?" Travis asked Baine.

"They drove a white Taurus rental car. I noticed because I'm thinking about trading mine in for one."

"You happen to remember their names?"

"Sorry." Baine shrugged.

"It's okay," Travis reassured him. "If they were thieves, I doubt they gave you their real names, anyway."

"They mentioned they were heading into town for lobster dinner. You might check the restaurants."

"Thanks, I'll do that." Travis handed Baine a business card. "If you think of anything else that might be helpful, please call. And we'd appreciate it if you didn't mention our conversation to anyone."

"No problem. Good luck finding your sister."

Sandy and Travis headed back to her car. Again, she let him drive. She was too tired to think straight, never mind argue, but she knew Travis well enough to know he was still upset with her.

He opened her door. After walking around the front of the car, he didn't even wait until he'd slipped into his seat and shut his door before admonishing her. "You could have been killed."

"Yeah."

"That was really dumb."

"Yeah."

Maybe if she kept agreeing with him, he'd stop trying to convince her she'd done the wrong thing. After all, no one had been shot. Baine hadn't called the police, and now they had a few leads—not good ones, but leads. While they couldn't be sure the men who had checked out the boat were the same ones who'd stolen her, the man who'd been driving Baine's boat had had a thick French accent. If they'd eaten dinner in town, maybe they'd left a credit card receipt. But the investigation was stalled for now. The restaurants wouldn't open until morning.

Travis would have to wait. He'd have to wait to follow up their leads, and he'd have to wait to harangue her. Sleepy, she closed her eyes and nodded off, right in the middle of their argument.

VANDERPELT LOOKED UP from the mountain of paperwork on his desk, disturbed by Alan's interruption, yet hopeful his employee brought him good news. "Has the woman found my boat?"

"Not yet."

"Then why are you here?" He'd made it clear to both his secretary and his bodyguard, outside the door, that he had important communications coming in by satellite link this morning. Vanderpelt's associates expected discretion, and would not be pleased if anyone overheard their private conversation.

"Ellie asked for some books to read."

"You bothered me for such inconsequential nonsense?" Despite Vanderpelt's fierce glare that would have silenced a lesser man, Alan continued as if he didn't fear his boss's displeasure.

His insubordination immediately drew Vanderpelt's attention. He was not a man to ignore details just because he preferred to concentrate on the big picture. Several immediate possibilities came to mind. Either he'd given Alan too much authority recently, and his underling felt he could question his boss, or guarding the woman prisoner was softening him.

Vanderpelt appreciated the woman's assets as much as other men did. Ellie Cantrel possessed the shapeliest pair of legs he'd seen this side of the silver screen.

However, Vanderpelt prided himself on his restraint. The business at hand would once again set America to lamenting. Careful planning would bring grief to the land of the infidel. This time, hundreds of thousands would die. Perhaps millions. And the American president would be forced to withdraw his troops from foreign soil.

"She's repeatedly asked to be taken outside to exercise." Alan kept his eyes respectfully downcast, his tone bland, but Vanderpelt didn't miss the veiled lust in his gaze. Clearly, Alan coveted the American woman.

"No." A man's passion and a woman's comfort were of no importance compared to Vanderpelt's plan. Besides, once her friend delivered his boat, they would all suffer a terrible accident at sea. Two women had no business sailing alone. To do so was foolhardy, and they would pay for their stupidity. "Is that all?"

"The real reason I'm here is that Sandy Vale's new mechanic is Ellie's brother, and he has a military background." Alan looked Vanderpelt straight in the eyes. "I thought you'd want to know."

"This man—"

"Travis Cantrel."

"I want to know everything about him before—"

Alan handed him a file. "I anticipated your request."

His underling might hold a soft spot in his heart for women, but the man was damned efficient. Alan Lavelle had moved up quickly through the ranks of Vanderpelt's organization due to his diligence and intelligence. Yet, Vanderpelt never quite trusted the man who had been born on French soil. But then again, Vanderpelt didn't trust anyone too much.

"When the time comes, you will make sure the three Americans die at sea."

"No problem." Alan didn't hesitate. The man might have a soft spot for women, but like any good soldier who followed orders, he would kill on Vanderpelt's command. And if he raped the women before they became fish food, Vanderpelt certainly wouldn't interfere—he believed in rewarding obedience.

Vanderpelt opened Travis Cantrel's file. The man had not been a particularly good student. As an average soldier, he'd served his time and been honorably discharged from the Army. He now repaired small engines for a firm in Connecticut. He'd never married or fathered children. He rented a one-bedroom apartment on the outskirts of town and drove a beat-up car that ran like new, no doubt due to his mechanical ability. He'd had four speeding tickets over the last ten years. And he had terrible credit, apparently spending the little he earned on women and the horses. Everything appeared...ordinary. On the surface, Travis Cantrel was no threat.

But Vanderpelt didn't wield the kind of power that gave minor despots nightmares by accepting surface reports. "I want you to dig deeper. Hire a private investigator to check out Mr. Cantrel."

Alan's eyes widened in surprise. "You see something wrong?"

Vanderpelt shook his head. "I like to be thorough. We

don't want any last-minute surprises. I especially want details about his army background."

"That's going to cost—"

"Bribe whomever you must."

"And it'll take some time."

"Have the information here before that man arrives with my boat."

Alan nodded. "They've found her?"

"Not yet." Vanderpelt's stomach clenched. He didn't like setbacks of any kind, and that boat was critical to his succcss.

"And if they don't find it?"

Vanderpelt didn't usually allow questions from subordinates. But he understood that for Alan to do his job well, he must anticipate his boss's needs. "There is no alternate plan. And failure is intolerable. If the Americans don't find my boat soon, perhaps we haven't given them enough incentive."

Alan's eyes narrowed. "What do you mean?"

"Send a tape of Ellie Cantrel to her friend. Slap her around a bit, first. Bloody her face. Have one of our associates special deliver it to the marina."

"I'm on it."

"Include another warning that contacting the authorities will lead to her death. And make sure there are no background clues in the tape."

"All right."

Vanderpelt returned to his paperwork, convinced the boat he needed would arrive soon. Meanwhile, he had other minutiae to check.

That's how he'd attained his position. By being careful. By always tying up his loose ends. Sandy, Ellie and Travis would not live long enough to learn their part in the betrayal of their country, or the massive destruction they'd helped to cause. Meanwhile, Vanderpelt ignored the irony of the American president searching overseas for weapons of mass destruction when one of them was already right under his nose. Just as they did on 9/11, the Americans would suffer a great blow. And Vanderpelt would go down in history as one of the world's great tactical masterminds.

Chapter Four

Ellie leafed through a magazine for the tenth time, her mind wandering to her dismal circumstances. The four walls felt as though they were closing in. Despite her efforts to remain upbeat, she'd never been kidnapped before, and was having difficulty controlling her fears.

She desperately wanted sunshine, fresh air and a change of clothing. Most of all, she wanted information.

Were her efforts to befriend her captor, Alan Lavelle, working? Alan brought her food and water twice a day. At first, he wouldn't talk to her or look at her. Not good. So she'd worked up a plan to make him see her as a person. Every time he entered her cell, she positioned herself in a different spot—one where he had to turn to find her.

He didn't talk much, but he seemed to listen when

she spoke. So she chatted about home and how much she longed to return to her life. She'd asked to go outside to exercise, and she'd pleaded for reading material to keep her mind occupied. Alan appeared to ignore her, but each time he stayed a bit longer, as if he couldn't help himself. And he must have listened, because he'd brought her magazines and several paperbacks.

Although he hadn't once allowed her out of her prison, Ellie kept working on him. Long before he arrived, she picked up the sound of Alan's approaching footsteps. Since it was not yet time for another meal, her hopes rose that he might be coming to let her out for exercise.

However, when he unlocked her door and peered inside, his face tight, his lips grim, her guts knotted. "What's wrong?"

He closed the door behind him, locked it and set up a camcorder on a tripod. "You and I are going to make a movie."

Oh, God. She'd wanted him to see her as a person, but not necessarily as a desirable female. She would have retreated, but she was already backed against the wall. Meanwhile, her thoughts raced, and panic galloped down her spine.

Alan might be medium height and build, but he was wiry. She recalled the strength of his grip when he'd kidnapped her from the sailboat, and knew he could overpower her in a heartbeat. Even if she could use the skills Travis had taught her to surprise him, retrieve the key and unlock her door, she doubted she could escape the island.

Mouth dry from fear, she forced herself to ask, "What kind of movie?"

"The kind where I slap you around."

She gasped, her stomach vaulting into her throat.

And Alan did the strangest thing. He placed a finger to his lips, as if fearing their conversation could be overheard. And he held up a bottle of ketchup. "Lady, when your friend sees our private movie," he said, pointing to the ketchup bottle, "blood spewing from your mouth, and hears your *screams* of pain, she's going to try much harder to find that boat."

Pain? Blood? Screams? Why had he emphasized the word *scream,* as if he was trying to send her a secret message?

What the hell was going on? And why was he still warning her not to speak with his finger over his lips? Was her cell bugged? Was someone listening just outside the door?

"Now, I get to tie you up."

"No."

"My boss isn't going to be happy unless he can hear some loud, piercing *screams.*"

"No!" She shouted, testing her theory that he wanted her to yell.

Alan motioned with his hands for her to scream some more. Ellie had no idea exactly what was going on, but she sensed that he might be trying to help her.

"Don't touch me, you bastard! Ouch! Stop it! No! Please! No more!"

Alan turned on the camcorder, then approached her

with a cord. He tied her hands so loosely that she understood this was for show. And when she pretended to struggle, screamed and kept her hands behind her back, he shot her an approving smile that the camera lens would never see.

Keeping his back to the camera and the ketchup bottle hidden, he smeared the red substance onto his palm. "Bitch." Raising his hand, he mouthed, "I'm sorry," and slapped her, smearing ketchup across her mouth.

Her cheeks stung, but Ellie understood he hadn't used all his strength, wouldn't use full force—unless she refused to cooperate. She snapped her head for the camera, making it appear he'd hit her harder than he actually had.

And she tried not to think about Sandy watching the tape. Prayed that her friend would somehow see through the farce that she was really okay.

Except Ellie wasn't okay. She'd been forced to play into some sick scenario that she didn't understand. She already knew that Sandy would be doing everything in her power to rescue her. Sending the tape and frightening her even more wasn't necessary.

The violence made her sick and shaky, but even as Alan slapped her again, she focused on helping herself. If anyone who knew her saw this tape, she wanted to send them a silent message. If her hands weren't supposed to be tied behind her back, she would have crossed her fingers—Travis and Ellie's childhood signal to one another that they were telling a lie. With her hands behind her back, Ellie did the next best thing. She crossed her legs and hoped the camera angle would capture her action.

Although she could have freed her hands, she didn't dare. With Alan screaming in her face, and her pleading with him to leave her alone, the scene was too stark, too close to real. Finally, he left, making no explanation. Shaken more than she wanted to admit, she washed the ketchup from her face. But she didn't stop trembling for a long, long time.

SANDY HEARD THE DOORBELL chime and tugged the pillow over her head. It was still dark—way too soon to think about crawling out of bed. Her eyelids stuck together, and a gritty taste in her mouth plus a groggy headache convinced her several more hours of sleep were necessary. But sleepy or not, once awakened, she couldn't turn off her thoughts. No one except Ellie ever rang her bell this early.

But Ellie was missing.

Maybe the cops had found the boat.

Tossing the pillow aside, she sat up too fast and had to wait for a slight dizziness to pass. Grabbing and donning her bathrobe, she slipped from her room before she came face-to-face with Travis, who'd slept in her spare bedroom.

With a five-o'clock shadow, no shirt and only boxers covering the essentials, he appeared more sexy than dangerous—despite the gun in his hand. No man should look so good this early in the morning. Between the fierce expression on his face, his penetrating dark eyes and his apparent readiness to fight, he held all the masculinity of a warrior setting off to battle. His scent was pure, primal male, and her body responded automatically—warmth pooling in her belly. With his bronzed chest, lightly dusted with curly hair, powerful neck and broad shoulders sloping to tautly drawn pectoral muscles and a flat, hard stomach, her mouth watered. Her fingers itched to touch the perfection of his flesh, but she forced her hands to clench her sash and draw the knot tighter.

The doorbell rang again.

"Maybe the cops found Vanderpelt's boat?" she said hopefully, her voice husky—from the lack of sleep. Yeah, right. Those mountains of perfect male flesh had nothing to do with the sexy yearning in her tone.

Travis shook his head and pointed the gun at the front door. "If the cops had found the boat, Kincaid would have called me."

"Maybe he was asleep."

"Kincaid never sleeps." Travis padded on bare feet over her tongue-and-groove oak floor, his footsteps silent.

"Everyone sleeps," she whispered, following right behind him, leaning so close she could feel heat radiating off his toned skin.

He peeked out the window. "No one's there. But there's a package on your front stoop."

"I'll get it."

"No." Setting the gun within easy reach on a shelf meant for knickknacks, he lifted an umbrella from its stand. Standing to one side of the door, he cracked it open, hooked the package with the umbrella handle and dragged it into the room.

"That's a priority mail postal envelope." She recognized the red, white and blue graphics, even in the dim light of the living area. "Usually my mailman comes at noon and delivers them directly to my mailbox."

Travis flipped the package over with the umbrella, taking care not to lean too close. "There's no stamp. The mailman didn't deliver this."

A chill of fear slid down her throat and settled in her gut. She didn't like being watched. She didn't like the people who took Ellie knowing where she lived. She didn't like how easily they'd invaded her world and turned it upside down. However, along with the fear came anger. She wanted to find Ellie and she wanted these people behind bars.

Frowning at the package, she took a cautious step closer. "Could it be a bomb?"

Travis shook his head. "A bomb would weigh more. It's too light."

Still, she noticed how he placed his body between her and the package before opening the pull tab and retrieving a videotape, touching only the edges. "I doubt we'll get prints, but maybe someone slipped up." He popped the tape into the VCR, turned on the television set and hit Play.

Ellie's face stared back at them. Was it the lighting, or had she already lost some of her deep tan? She still wore the same clothes in which she'd been abducted. For a moment, a man's back blocked their view of Ellie.

Although his face wasn't shown, Sandy recognized Alan from his silhouette and the way he moved. "That's Alan Lavelle, Vanderpelt's man who sailed with us back to the States."

When Alan raised his hand and struck Ellie, splitting her lip and leaving a bloody smear on her face, Sandy's stomach contracted. When Ellie screamed in pain and fear, the nausea in Sandy's stomach expanded up her throat, constricting her vocal cords until she felt as if she couldn't suck air into her lungs.

Sagging onto the sofa, Sandy could barely make herself watch the sickening scene. Poor Ellie. They had to find that boat and rescue her. Those sick bastards had no reason to hurt her. None.

Aching to yell at Travis to turn off the violence and turn down the sound, she bit hard on her lip instead. They needed to watch the entire tape. Maybe they could glean clues as to where Vanderpelt was holding Ellie. Maybe she might say something that could help them find her. But as Alan struck Ellie again and her head snapped sideways, flinging blood onto the wall, Travis leaned forward, his tone excited. "This might be a break."

Startled that Travis didn't seem too upset, she frowned at him, glad to have an excuse to watch anything other than Ellie being beaten. By the end of the short tape, she would have expected Travis to be pacing, cursing, livid at what his sister had had to endure. But his reaction was focused, and difficult for Sandy to read, especially with her own confused emotions kicking in.

Saying the words aloud was an effort. "What are you talking about? That man is beating Ellie."

"No. He isn't." Travis rewound the tape. He restarted it, but this time played it in slow motion. "Watch carefully. Ellie is anticipating the blows, turning her head from him at the last second."

"So, she'd avoiding pain. I don't see..." But Sandy forced herself to watch the timing closely. Travis was correct. Ellie was avoiding most of the beating.

Travis froze the tape. "Look closely. Do you see a cut on her face? Do you see her lips swelling?"

"The blood may be hiding—"

"That's not blood. The consistency is wrong."

"What are you saying?"

"That someone wants us to think they are torturing Ellie—but they aren't."

"That's twisted."

"No, it's good. Either Ellie has found someone to help her from the inside, or whoever took her really doesn't want to hurt her."

Sandy supposed Travis was making sense, but she was having trouble thinking without caffeine to kick-start her brain. She stood up and entered the kitchen to make coffee. She took down two mugs and placed coffee bags inside with hot water, placed them in the microwave and set the timer. "Then why send the tape? What's the point?"

"To scare us? To make us work harder to find her?" Travis checked the envelope, and a typed note on plain bond paper slid out. Again, he held it up just by the edges. "It's another warning not to bring in the authorities."

She shivered, frozen in fear for Ellie. Those men holding her could do whatever they wanted to her. They could hurt her for real, rape her, toss her into the ocean afterwards, and no one would ever be able to prove a thing. Travis might believe the tape was a good sign, but it had simply reminded Sandy how helpless they were to stop these men.

The microwave must have dinged but she never heard it. Travis came up beside her, removed the two mugs and thrust one into her hands. "Drink."

Her hands shook so hard, Sandy almost dropped the cup. Travis immediately placed his arm around her and led her back to the sofa, where he pulled her beside him. Resting her head on his shoulder, she leaned on his quiet strength.

"Ellie is strong. She's going to be fine. I don't even think her hands were tied behind her back. The whole thing was staged. Badly staged. I think whoever filmed this wanted us to realize that the entire scene was faked."

"But—"

"Did you see Ellie cross her legs? Her move was deliberate. She was telling me not to believe the lie." Travis's palm rubbed up and down Sandy's shoulder, creating a warming friction, but it didn't reach deep enough.

She sipped her coffee and set the mug on the coffee table. When she leaned back, Travis tugged her onto his lap and she cuddled against his chest, her forehead resting in the curve of his neck. "I'm so sorry I got her into this mess."

"Hey, don't go blaming yourself. No way is this your fault."

"I was the one who talked her into going into the marina as partners. I was the one who took Vanderpelt's commission from Danzler."

"And I taught Ellie to sail. Does that mean this is my fault?" Travis's question was rhetorical. His arms closed around Sandy. When he held her so tight, his heat penetrated the places he touched, but the rest of her still trembled with cold. "Let's be clear. The people to blame are the men who took Ellie. Not you. Not me. We have enough to deal with without your making yourself sick with guilt." His hands rubbed her back, then one hand tilted her jaw upward, until their gazes tangled. "You okay?"

"I will be." The heat in his look stole her breath, but warmed her soul. The searing self-assurance in his eyes was the man she remembered. He'd never lost that cocky edge, but now his confidence was tempered by compassion. The old Travis had blamed Sandy every time Ellie came back late from a date. But the new Travis understood more than Sandy had ever imagined. She liked this new Travis. She liked him a lot.

"Hold that thought." As if reading her mind, he grinned—a charming smile that reminded her of the boy who'd too often depended on charm, rather than substance, to convince her of his intentions.

"What thought?"

"The thought that's making your eyes dilate and your pulse race."

She tried to pull back but he wouldn't let her. "I don't want you anymore, Travis."

"Yes. You do." He chuckled then, and she wanted to smack him. No one could make her as hot or as angry as Travis. It was her curse. Why couldn't she find a levelheaded man, one who didn't think he was the cat's meow, one who didn't pour himself into boxers like some elegant James Bond-type and remind her of sex on the beach every time she looked at him?

"But we have work to do." He kissed her lightly on the lips, then dumped her from his lap to the sofa. "I have to find a pay phone to call Kincaid, arrange for a team to pick up this tape. Experts might get prints off it, or perhaps glean more information from details we missed."

She reached for her coffee cup, pretending that Travis had no effect on her whatsoever. "While you do that, I'll check with the local marinas and coast guards. Maybe someone has found Vanderpelt's boat."

Travis stood as if he meant to go off just then, but he stopped. And the temper he'd kept caged pawed through the bars.

Moments ago, Travis had seemed to want to go straight to work. He'd dumped her from his lap, albeit gently, but now she realized something else was on his mind. "Before we get to work, we have one other thing to discuss."

Uh-oh. She knew that tone of voice. The I'm-trying-to-be-patient tone he used right before his temper exploded. She gazed at him, suddenly wary. "Yes?"

"Last night you fell asleep on the way home—"

"Is that a complaint?" she teased, stalling for time. She didn't want to argue. She knew he disapproved of her actions at Baine's house and she didn't want to discuss them. Obviously, he couldn't let it go.

"You were clearly exhausted, and I didn't want to burden you with more stress last night."

She raised her eyebrow. "And now?"

"Now, I no longer have a choice."

She folded her arms across her chest and tried to keep her voice even. "I did what I thought was right."

"That's the problem."

How could just three little words make her so angry? Travis had always known how his sarcasm got under her skin, using just the right intonation to inflame her. "I acted to save you from being shot. And it worked."

He scowled down at her. "That doesn't make you right."

She stood, physically lessening the distance between them, balancing on her toes like a prize fighter coming out of the corner at the bell, ready and willing not only to defend herself, but attack. But Travis remained tall enough to still glare down at her. Lifting her chin, she locked gazes with him. "You never liked a woman who could think independently."

"That's not true." He threaded his fingers through his hair. "Last night, you promised to let me call the shots and then you disregarded that promise."

"The situation changed." She didn't comprehend why Travis had to make a fuss. After all these years, she would have thought he'd had more self-esteem than to take it so personally when she made a decision without consulting him first. "Baine was holding a gun on you. If I hadn't stepped in, Baine would certainly have called the cops, and he might have shot you."

"I was behind a car and protected. You put yourself in danger, at his mercy."

Travis always could argue well, but she couldn't help thinking that the real reasons for his annoyance were threefold—that she'd gone back on her word, that she'd thought for herself and that her decision had been a good one. "My coming out of the shadows stopped him from shooting at you."

Travis shook his head, his tone fierce and insistent. "He didn't shoot because he's a good guy." Travis glared at her. "By disregarding my orders, you walked into the open. *You* could have been shot."

"It was my decision, my life." Sandy didn't like this Travis. He wasn't yelling at her, but dressing her down as if she was ignorant, and he was saddled with an incompetent partner.

"Stepping out of the darkness was foolhardy. You didn't just risk your own life. If Baine had panicked and aimed at you, I would have had to shoot *him.*"

"I...didn't think...of that." Baine's safety had never crossed her mind. After all, he'd been the one holding the gun. As much as she didn't want to admit it, she supposed Travis had a point. For the first time since the incident last night, she questioned her actions. If she'd stayed hidden, as Travis had requested, he might have talked Baine out of shooting by himself. There may have been no need for her to step into the picture. In the split second she'd taken to decide, she'd failed to consider all the possible scenarios and implications, as Travis may have. She'd known she wasn't the expert here, he was. From his perspective, he had every right to be annoyed with her.

And she had to give him credit. Not only wasn't he yelling, he'd actually waited to discuss his displeasure after she'd had a night's rest. The least she could do was act as maturely.

"I'm sorry."

His eyes flared. "I couldn't bear to lose Ellie and you, too."

"I'll be more careful next time."

"Damn it. Next time, you'll do what I tell you."

Without agreeing to his last statement, she turned and went to dress. Travis might have learned to hide his temper, but it was still there, firing just below the surface, ready to ignite. His frustration with her was very clear, but it was the glimpse of pain in his eyes and the gentleness in his tone when he'd declared that he couldn't bear to lose her, too, that got to her.

She tried to tell herself that Travis was referring to the closeness they'd once shared. That his statement had nothing to do with the present. And yet...was she simply fooling herself? Could two people who had shared the kind of passion they once had ever truly work together without some of the old feelings flaring anew?

Their fights over Ellie had driven a permanent wedge

between them. How ironic if now concern and love for Ellie drew Sandy and Travis back together. The twenty-two-year-old Travis had been unprepared to raise the rebellious seventeen-year-old that Ellie had been. When Travis came down on her too hard, restricting Ellie's every attempt to have fun and forget the pain of losing their parents, Sandy had tried to mediate.

Their parents' fatal accident had made Ellie more determined to live life, experiment and have fun. And Travis had been just as determined to keep the last remaining member of his family protected and safe. Both sister and brother had been right, and wrong. Sandy had often tried to settle their arguments, asking each of them to compromise. Ellie had appreciated her efforts. Travis hadn't.

When Travis couldn't repress Ellie's wild spirit, he'd come close to smothering her in overprotective love. He'd tried to chase away the boys who clamored for Ellie's attention. He'd tried to limit her friends to those of whom he approved. Worst of all, his actions born out of love had been driving Ellie away, making her even more rebellious.

Sandy had tried to arbitrate their fights. She saw no harm in Ellie's piercing her ears or dating local boys. But when Ellie had wanted to pierce other body parts, Sandy had sided with Travis. And she'd helped Ellie shop for attractive clothes, but Travis had still found them too revealing. When Sandy had tried to get Ellie to tone down the makeup that Travis thought made her look too grown-up, Ellie simply applied more once she left the house.

Meanwhile, Travis believed Sandy was undermining his authority instead of trying to help. The arguments came to a head one night when Ellie went out on a date and didn't come home until morning.

Travis had been frantic with worry. And when Sandy finally admitted to him that Ellie was seeing a boy he didn't approve of, Travis had gone ballistic—especially after he found out Sandy didn't have a clue where they'd gone. It seemed to Sandy that Travis only wanted her opinion when she agreed with him. He'd been furious that she hadn't told him about Ellie's new boyfriend, even after she'd pointed out that if he'd had a better relationship with his sister, Ellie would have been able to tell him herself, instead of keeping secrets.

And when a radiant Ellie had returned home the next morning after spending an entire night with the boy, Travis hadn't been able to forgive Sandy. Things between them had never again been the same. Travis kept expecting her to undermine his authority, and she couldn't live life on the edge of his temper, always wondering when he would explode next.

For her own peace of mind, she'd left him. And he may not have ever forgiven her for that, either. Ellie had told her it had taken him a long time to recover. But it had taken her a long time to get over Travis, too.

Sandy had dated many men since then. She'd had a few lovers. But none of the men could ever compare to the larger-than-life image of Travis. Because, although things between them had been bad, they'd also been more than good. Travis loved the sea as much as she did.

They'd shared a connection to the outdoors and to adventure that she'd never felt so strongly with anyone else.

But that connection worried her. If she got too close, she'd once again be burned. Been there, done that. She wouldn't make the same mistake again.

Chapter Five

Although most restaurants weren't open to customers in the morning, as early risers, Travis and Sandy would be able to meet fishermen coming in from sea with their catch and local restaurant owners who'd buy the catch. A thriving fish market brought together sport fisherman, commercial fishermen, wholesale buyers, that included food packagers as well as restaurant owners, and assorted service people hawking their wares. Unfortunately, it was unlikely that a chef or entrepreneur would have also doubled as a waiter or waitress and would recall serving a customer with a French accent.

But Travis wanted to get out of Sandy's house for several reasons. The tension between them would lessen with a good airing out. He needed to make those phone calls and use a "dead drop" to pass the videotape to one of Kincaid's experts, who would pick up the tape from under Sandy's front porch steps. Besides, cabin fever had set in.

Although he'd known within moments of viewing the tape that the entire incident had been staged, and he welcomed anyone who might be helping Ellie from inside Vanderpelt's organization, the tape was a vivid reminder that they needed to find Ellie quickly. Travis drove past the first pay phone, and left Sandy in the car while he phoned Kincaid from a breakfast diner.

After speaking with his boss, Travis felt more settled, more focused on business. And he was finally able to put aside the personal animosity between him and Sandy. While Sandy was a go-with-the-flow person, Travis felt restless when he didn't know exactly where he stood. The mix of leftover passion, old resentments and hurt feelings, plus the mutual worry over Ellie, had him on edge, distracting him from focusing solely on his sister. But talking to his boss tended to keep him on track, especially with the blitz of new information coming their way.

One of the main reasons he'd joined the Shey Group was Logan Kincaid. The man had a reputation for taking care of his team—not just paying them well, but looking out for their well-being. He spared no expense to buy the best equipment or hire the most qualified specialist. But what bred loyalty was his leave-no-man-behind-and-no-clue-unchecked motto.

As soon as Kincaid had learned about Ellie's disappearance, he'd willingly thrown his resources into helping Travis. And those resources were some of the best intelligence money could buy. Between Kincaid's CIA connections, that extended from the White House to the Kremlin, and his current network of Shey operatives, he had considerable pull. While many of the Shey Group were posted elsewhere on assignments, just one hour of time from a man like Ryker Stevens could be priceless. The computer genius had programs scrutinizing police, as well as Navy and Coast Guard databases in search of the missing boat. At the same time, he'd done a deep intel search into Vanderpelt's background.

Travis rejoined Sandy in the car. "Kincaid is sending us a special package at the marina."

"What kind of package?" Sandy asked, seeming as willing to put the personal things aside as Travis was, for now. Their earlier discussion had left her subdued, but he hoped she'd heeded his words because he needed her cooperation. For once, she had to accept that he knew what he was doing.

"Cash. Fake IDs for both of us."

"Why would we need those?"

"We probably won't. There's also satellite phone systems. Decryption equipment. Guns. Ammo. Tear gas. Bulletproof vests. Lock picks. C-4. Dynamite. Timers. Medical kits. Emergency flares."

Her eyes rounded. "What does all that gear cost?"

"Lots. But it's a standard package, modified to our needs. Kincaid doesn't skimp on equipment. He'd rather overdo, and save his men, than send them out in the field without apparatus that could keep them alive. But best of all, he's got intel on Vanderpelt."

"Does he know if Ellie's on the island?"

Travis shook his head. "Satellite photos have seen no sign of her. That could mean she's not there, or that they are keeping her inside, or that the hourly overhead flyby shots missed her."

"So what *do* we know?"

He heard disappointment in her tone, and swung onto the highway. "Don't be discouraged. The way investigations work is like a puzzle. We collect little pieces, then the corners and the edges fit together before we can guess at the missing middle. Even the lack of intel on Vanderpelt is helpful."

"Why?"

"Because we are now fairly certain his identity is a deep cover."

"Do we know who he really is?"

"Kincaid, and Ryker—the Shey Group's computer specialist—are working on it.

"But knowing Vanderpelt is undercover tells us that he's *not* an eccentric, wealthy citizen who simply wants his boat. The background on his childhood is scarce. He never attended the private British school he claims. We're not even sure where he's from."

"So if he's been undercover for years, how do you find out? I'd imagine after such a long time that he's covered his tracks well."

"We trace his associates, his phone calls, his travels and, most especially, we follow the money trail. We want to know who he does business with, where he makes his money and where it's funneled. Certain organizations are fronts for terrorists. Sometimes despots or dictators of Asian, South American or Middle Eastern countries steal billions of dollars from their people by hiding multinational corporations under secret identities."

"But why would any of them want Ellie?"

"We don't know." Leave it to Sandy to cut right to the heart of the problem. Travis checked the rearview mirror for a tail then returned his gaze to the curvy road. "Maybe Ellie saw something that she considered insignificant but that would give away a secret. However, since they haven't killed her, we can discount that possibility."

"Why else would Ellie be important to anyone?"

"Vanderpelt may know about the Shey Group—which is unlikely, but always possible. Perhaps he wants me for some reason and is using Ellie to lure me to the island."

Sandy peered at him through narrowed eyes. "What kind of missions do you do, Travis?"

"I can't be specific. Last month I guarded the friend of someone being blackmailed. Before that I helped rescue one of the Shey Group, who'd been captured and was being tortured." Satisfaction entered his tone. "We foiled a plan to set off bombs throughout the U.S. on Independence Day. Since 9/11, our intelligence agencies have gone into high alert. Americans are safer because many good people behind the scenes put their lives on the line every day."

"You sound content."

"What's not to like about my work? I'm on a team with a great bunch of dedicated people. I travel all over the world, and I'm paid well."

"And the work is dangerous."

"True, but I make up for that with skill."

"Do you really think your work has put Ellie in danger?" Sandy asked, sounding hesitant to cast blame when he'd so clearly told her how much he enjoyed what he did. But the option had to be explored because Ellie was a likely pawn in a much bigger picture.

"I don't know. But I assure you, my contacts are being cross-matched against Vanderpelt's people. Ryker's program will eventually tell us what we need to know. Meanwhile, we should focus on tracking down the men who abducted Ellie, because I'd hate to find the boat, sail to the island, and then find out that she's not there and that Vanderpelt is holding her elsewhere."

"You said Kincaid has contacts. Couldn't we find a legitimate reason to inspect the island?"

Travis shook his head. "That would simply put them on guard. Besides, if Ellie is there, they'd keep her hidden. However, Kincaid did say that he's found one of the men who built Vanderpelt's dock. It's only a matter of time before we have maps and a tactical plan."

He pulled into the local fish market parking lot, surprised at its growth during his absence. What had once been a few local fishermen and restauranteurs had expanded into a thriving center of commerce. With the ocean breeze blowing, the scent of fish was present but not overly strong. Dock workers loaded ocean-caught fish, such as tuna, cod, haddock, mackerel and striped bass, into refrigerated trucks. Fisherman also sold freshwater catches, such as brook trout, white perch and pickerel, to an assortment of wholesale buyers. Hungry seagulls circled overhead and dived for scraps, their caws adding to the auctioneer's patter. Tourists eyeballed the assortment of goods while grocers packed shipments onto ice-laden trucks, to haul and resell later in the day.

During high school, Travis had worked part-time for a restaurant, and he vividly recalled the section reserved for locals who often chose the prime pick of the day's catch. He headed in that direction. "The economy appears to be booming."

"With more Americans vacationing at home, our businesses have picked up much of the tourism slack from the northeast corridor. More people eat fish now, as part of their diets, instead of just chicken and beef."

Sandy walked beside him, clearly at home in the masculine environment. Many of the fishermen waved to her and gave Travis a scrutinizing once-over, as if he was a stranger instead of a natural-born native. The community might have grown, but the native New Englanders' mistrust of outsiders hadn't changed. Up here, people looked out for their own. But they also minded their business. Most of these folks would have heard about the stolen boat, and would keep their eyes and ears open for news, but they wouldn't intrude on Sandy's privacy or question her without good reason.

Between the salt air, the fresh breeze and Sandy's

hand in his, Travis slowly relaxed. Last night's tense encounter with Baine followed by this morning's videotape and the argument with Sandy had him too keyed up. Searching for clues took patience. Trying to go too fast might only cause him to exhaust himself and overlook something vital. During the years he'd worked in the military, and later for the Shey Group, he'd learned that staying sharp, taking time to eat and sleep, might be as critical to success as mastering the art of patience. No matter how much he longed to rush and question every restaurant owner on the dock, he took time to breathe, to let the wind clear his head and to savor a simple walk through a favorite site from his youth.

"There's Merle Casset from the Rocky Inn. We might save ourselves some time by talking to her." Sandy pointed out the biggest gossip this side of the Atlantic. Gray-haired, sharp-eyed, Merle Casset had run the inn since her husband had made her a widow. He'd been lost at sea during a storm, over two decades ago, leaving her alone with five kids to raise. Merle had single-handedly kept the place going, and could have written the newspaper's society column—if their small town had had any celebrities. Instead, she kept track of marriages, deaths and births as closely as the local retirees watched the stock market.

"Good suggestion." After coming down so hard on Sandy for her actions last night, Travis tried to be fair and give compliments when they were due. He didn't want to discourage ideas, he just wanted her to share them before she acted.

As if seeing right through him, Sandy frowned. "I'm not that fragile. I goofed up last night, but that doesn't mean I'm agreeing that you always know best."

"Of course I always know best," he teased. "I'm perfect."

"Perfect to look at, maybe." Merle interrupted their conversation as if this wasn't the first contact she'd had with Travis in years. "But I suspect that hot temper makes you next to impossible to live with." She chuckled, then turned her attention to Sandy. "What can I do to help?"

"We're looking for a thief." Sandy didn't want the locals to know Ellie was missing—someone might alert the authorities—so she'd made up a story. "We think he had a strong French accent and planned to eat a lobster dinner last Thursday night."

Merle's bushy, gray brows narrowed. "That's not much to go on. I haven't heard of any Frenchman in the area."

"He's probably long gone," Travis told her.

"However, both the Garden and the Sea Mist have lobster specials on Thursday night. You might check there first, and you might sit down and have a good meal, Sandy—you look thin enough that a strong gale could blow you away."

"Thanks, Merle." Sandy kissed the widow's cheek in an open display of affection—rare in the area—while Travis tried to decide if there was merit to Merle's observation. Since he hadn't seen Sandy in years, he didn't know her normal weight, but she looked like the same slim girl he remembered. However, the dark circles under her eyes attested to sleepless nights, and he vowed to look after her better as Sandy continued, "And we'll keep searching for the thief—so if you hear anything at all..."

"I've got your cell number. You sure you're not interested in my Harry? He may not be so pretty—" she glanced at Travis, eyes teasing "—but he's the calm sort. Reliable. Makes a good living and knows how to feed a woman. He doesn't go gallivanting all over the world to—"

"Merle," Sandy interrupted, "we really need to get going." Sandy tugged Travis by the hand, and he allowed her to drag him away from the friendly widow. "So now what?" she asked. "Do we hang around here and ask more questions, or head out to the restaurants?"

Travis checked his watch, wondering if there had ever been anything between Harry Casset and Sandy. She'd sure drawn him away from Merle in a hurry. But, then again, they didn't have time to stand and gossip all morning. "Let's go talk to the waiters and waitresses before they're hit with the lunchtime crowd."

THE MOMENT TRAVIS STARTED the car, and he had Sandy trapped where avoiding him would be difficult, he asked about Harry. "It's hard for me to believe that you were ever interested in Harry Casset."

"Who says I was?" Sandy attempted to keep her voice light and playful, and contained a sigh of annoyance at his underhanded tactic, but sensed she'd failed miserably on all counts.

"Fine. We don't have to talk about him. It's none of my business."

"Damn straight." Annoyed that she felt so defensive, Sandy pronged her fingers through her hair to straighten the tangles from the wind. Travis had been away for years. He had no right to ask questions about her personal life. And yet, she couldn't help the little jiggle of pleasure coursing through her that he was curious. "Harry Casset and I had exactly one dinner together. It was a disaster. He wants someone who reads literature, who watches movies with subtitles and who has a Ph.D. in keeping Harry's home neat and clean. I didn't fit the bill." She let out a snort at the memory, then grinned. "As he put it, we didn't 'suit.'"

Travis chuckled. "I couldn't envision a less likely pair than you and Harry. The man is so conservative as to be stodgy. But I imagine you don't spend any more time alone than you wish."

"You're prying. Again."

He shot her a charming glance. "Is curiosity a crime?"

"Only if you don't mind answering some questions of mine." She could have sworn he winced. Travis wasn't a man to kiss and tell, or brag. He was the kind of man every girl would want for a fling. Sexy. Charming. Dangerous. Good as hell in bed. But husband material? She'd rather settle down with a porcupine. "I've had two serious relationships since we parted. One was the local veterinarian, the other a stockbroker who keeps a summer home."

"And?"

"It's your turn."

"Almost my turn. What went wrong?"

"The stockbroker didn't spend enough time in Maine, and we more or less drifted apart due to lack of interest. The vet was on the rebound from a divorce. He eventually married his assistant." And she'd been relieved after she had moved on. Neither man had been exactly right for her, and just because she'd turned thirty, she wasn't willing to settle. "Now, it's your turn," she insisted.

"There's been no one special in my life."

No big surprise there. Travis didn't stay in one place long enough to form attachments.

"No one special…since you," he amended, throwing a little zing down her spine that she refused to classify. "I guess you were right when you told me that you were the best thing that ever happened to me, and that I was an overbearing jackass who couldn't appreciate you since I was an idiot."

"What?" She didn't recall saying any such things. For a moment, he had her going, before she realized he was teasing again.

"And since you couldn't win an argument with a stupid, stubborn, nonsupportive sexist like me, you weren't going to try. So after dicing and slicing my heart, you stormed out of my life and left me to put myself back together."

She chuckled at his melodrama. "I was so bad that it's a wonder you still speak to me."

"I have fond memories of you when you were bad."

"Travis—"

"And wonderful memories of when you were good."

"Don't—"

"I didn't even mind you when you were mad," he kept teasing, just to see if he could still make her squirm, she was sure of it. "And I especially looked forward to making up."

In bed. That's where they always made up. Between the sheets, under the sheets, on top of the sheets. Sometimes, they didn't make it to the sheets.

She shoved the memories aside. Back then they'd been kids with uncontrollable hormones. Of course, the sex had been blazing hot and as important to her as drawing her next breath. However, she was no longer so impressionable, no longer so eager to take on the challenge that was Travis. He was simply too much work. She didn't want a man she had to change. She wanted one who fit into her lifestyle, who wouldn't say *red* just because she said *green.*

"Turn right at the corner." She changed the subject as they neared their destination.

"I know where the Sea Mist is—unless the entire restaurant has relocated since the last time I was here."

"You were going so fast, I thought you might miss the turn."

He peered at her, his tone sounding genuinely puzzled. "I was driving below the speed limit."

She checked the speedometer to see that, once again, he was correct. It wasn't his driving that was going too fast, but her heart rate. His teasing had always had that effect on her. At least she no longer blushed like she once did—now *that* would be embarrassing.

The Sea Mist restaurant was run by Don Macary and his son, Little Don. They'd been serving up lobster specials on Thursday nights for as long as Sandy could remember. Her folks had brought her here to celebrate her tenth birthday. That night had been special, but couldn't compare to her first date here with Travis. She'd felt all grown-up, drinking her first glass of wine, gazing into Travis's eyes over a candlelit table. She'd never forget the taste of the sweet, succulent lobster, drizzled with heated butter, or the bold heat in his eyes that made her feel yummier than the twice-baked potatoes and clam chowder, which had been nothing short of divine. To banish the memory of Travis, she reminded herself that she'd eaten recently with her folks, who were currently on an RV trip to Alaska, and she made a mental note to take them to dinner when they returned.

Perched on the hillside and overlooking the ocean, the restaurant's front parking lot was currently empty. But Little Don was just climbing up from the wine cellar and waving a bottle at them. "Hi, Sandy. Travis, I heard you were back."

"We're looking for two thieves," Sandy told him. "They may have eaten here last Thursday night. One of them had a thick French accent."

Little Don, who must have weighed over three hundred pounds, frowned. "I filled in for Jeffrey, my normal waiter that night. I don't recall anyone with a French accent, but we were swamped." He turned toward the kitchen and bellowed. "Sheila!"

"Coming." A moment later, a slim, young woman bustled out of the kitchen, a stack of linen tablecloths over one shoulder, crystal salt and pepper shakers on a tray in her hands. "Yes?"

"Last Thursday night, during the lobster special, do you recall a Frenchman?"

Sheila set down the tray and linens, her brows drawn in thought. "Yeah, I do."

"Did he pay by credit card?" Travis asked her. "We believe he might be a thief."

Sheila shook her head. "He paid in cash. Left a small tip. I wish I could help. I'm sorry."

"Do you recall hearing any of their conversation while you served them?" Travis asked.

Knowing how unlikely it would be for a busy waitress to recall anything pertinent, Sandy held her breath.

"Sorry. It was hectic that night." Sheila's eyes suddenly widened. "But one of the men left an unusual matchbook on the table—and I collect them." She stepped behind the front desk, retrieved her purse and pawed inside it. "I may still have it. Here." She held the matchbook toward Travis, her tone triumphant. "You can keep it if you like."

"Are you sure it came from their table?" Sandy asked.

"I'm sure."

Travis took the matchbook from Sheila and shot her a grin. "It's from the Friendly Whale Bed-and-Breakfast. This could be just what we need. Thanks."

"You're welcome." Sheila smiled at Travis, clearly interested in him. "Let me know how it turns out."

Travis might not have had any serious relationships in the last ten years, but clearly he still attracted women. Hell, any female would have to have stopped breathing not to notice his handsome face, and Sandy couldn't hold the mild flirtation against the girl. She had no claim on Travis.

Yet for all his faults and all his flightiness, Travis had never been unfaithful. When they were together, they'd been together. That he'd moved on so easily while she'd spent years recovering was simply due to her own crushed dreams. She'd thought Travis was forever. She'd thought they'd found true love. She'd thought wrong.

The bed-and-breakfast was up in the hills. An old Victorian that had been restored with loving care over the last decade, it had four rooms on the second and third floors for guests. Such a small place didn't usually hand out matchbooks, but the previous owners had recently retired to Florida, and the new ones from New York City were promotion-minded. They even had an upscale Web site.

While both of the new owners and the maid all remembered the French gentleman, again Sandy and Travis heard how he'd paid cash, and had likely registered under an alias. They'd turned up nothing new. Discouraged, she tried to recall Travis likening the search to a puzzle. But, damn, they needed more pieces. While Travis drove them back to town, she played absently with the matchbook. The pretty picture of the Victorian bed-and-breakfast reminded her that they'd come up empty there. She flipped it over and spied writing on the back.

"Travis, look. Someone wrote a phone number on the back of this matchbook. There's even an area code."

"Where?"

"I don't know. It's not local."

"Good work. I'll have Kincaid trace the number, but try not to get your hopes up. We don't know if the men who took Ellie wrote that number down, or if it will lead to anything."

"I know, I know." But she couldn't stop her rising hopes and excitement.

Chapter Six

Travis stopped to phone Kincaid, and wondered if he'd picked up another tail. If so, he wasn't concerned. With Kincaid's encryption system, the call was safe. However, while he spoke he kept a close watch on Sandy. He'd already lost Ellie, and he didn't want the tail to so much as approach her.

He read the phone number on the matchbook to Kincaid and then listened to news. By the time the conversation ended, Kincaid had traced the phone number and given him useful information. Hurrying back to Sandy in the car, Travis reminded himself that before they followed up the new lead, he needed to feed her. And his growling stomach wouldn't mind lunch, either.

After they'd stopped to eat garlic-braised grouper

sandwiches and sip thick, chocolate shakes at a local watering hole, he gave Sandy the good news. "Kincaid traced the phone number to what we believe is Vanderpelt's private line. The bright spot is that once we had the phone number, we found many calls between Vanderpelt and Bayside. Our Frenchman goofed up twice and used his cell phone to call Vanderpelt. And after Ellie disappeared, the phone calls between the Frenchman's private cell phone and Vanderpelt's private line stopped."

"You think Ellie is definitely on Vanderpelt's island, and that's why there have been no more calls between the two men?" Sandy glanced at him. "And you've known this since before lunch and didn't tell me?"

"I was waiting for the right moment. There's more."

"What?" Her tone was sharp and eager.

"Kincaid says Canadian fishermen found the boat on their side of the border."

Sandy punched him in the shoulder. "Travis, if you hold back on me again, I swear the next punch will either break my fist or your jaw. Why the hell didn't you tell me sooner? We shouldn't have eaten. We could have been… Where is the boat?"

Travis rubbed his sore shoulder. Sandy might not know how to fight dirty, like Ellie, but nevertheless her punch packed a wallop. "That's precisely why I made you eat first. You would have wanted to drive over to the flats right away—"

"Exactly." Sandy eyed him as if he were crazy. "Must I remind you that we don't have a lot of time here? And there's no telling what Ellie might be going through."

"I know." Travis clenched the steering wheel tightly. Sandy knew how to strike with words as well as with her fists. He accepted the slashing pain of concern for Ellie, then locked it down hard. "But if we go without food or sleep, when we finally get to the island, we'll be of no use to her."

"I'm sorry." Sandy wearily rubbed her forehead. "I know you're worried about her. I shouldn't have... It seems as if I'm always apologizing. Perhaps I'm *not* thinking so clearly."

"Kincaid verified that the videotape was faked. The blood was likely watered-down ketchup. While we haven't ascertained exactly how Alan fits into Vanderpelt's organization, we have to assume that Ellie is going to be okay with his help. I must believe that to keep going."

Sandy eyed him with concern, her anger muted. "But, we should get to the hull as soon as possible. You had no right to hold back that information."

"The Canadians located the boat aground near Baybridge. We can't get to the hull until the next low tide." Travis reached over and squeezed Sandy's hand. "We have time. And you need to keep up your strength. We both do."

"All right. You've made your point. If I promise to eat, you have to promise not to hold back information. Deal?"

"Deal."

They shook hands. And he couldn't quite believe

they'd come to a compromise without shouting. Then again, he'd do anything for Ellie, and so would Sandy.

Obviously Sandy's mind was working in a different direction. "Did Kincaid say what kind of shape the boat's in?"

"The bow smashed into rocks before she grounded on the sandbar. The engine's likely been underwater for days."

"Can you reconstruct her?"

"Yeah, with enough tools, enough time and enough spare parts. It might end up being easier to simply scrap the old engine and put in a new one."

"I'll leave that decision up to you. Is the mast gone?"

"Yup. And the hull's cracked down to the keel."

Sandy cursed under her breath. "This is going to be expensive. I have a credit line on my house and a little money in the bank. If we hadn't just refurbished the forklift—"

"I've got the money angle covered. Don't worry about it." Travis had saved almost every dime Kincaid had ever paid him. He wasn't cheap. However, on a mission, there was little opportunity to spend his pay. And over the past five years, he'd taken one mission after another without much downtime. The end result was a tidy nest egg stashed in the stock market and real estate investments, as well as bank accounts in Switzerland, the Cayman Islands and New York. Travis had plenty to refurbish a fleet of boats, with enough left over to never work another day if he so chose.

"I'm paying half," Sandy insisted.

"Okay." He agreed because to do otherwise would

hurt her self-respect. Sandy took immense pride in supporting herself, building her marina and being self-sufficient. But Travis knew how to cook the books, knew how to pay people so she'd never guess the real costs. He had no intention of allowing her to put her home in jeopardy when he could so easily afford this undertaking. And he refused to argue when going behind her back was easier. Of course, she might eventually find out. But he grinned as he recalled how much he enjoyed making up after one of their arguments.

She glared at him. "What's so funny?"

"Nothing."

"Travis—"

"Do you want me to lie?"

She scowled at him. "I want the truth."

"I was just recalling how we made up after one of our arguments."

"Travis!" Her eyes widened, then narrowed. Her mouth snapped shut, and she stared straight ahead at the road. Once, she would have blushed. Now, she simply closed down on him, so that he couldn't tell what she was thinking.

"You said you wanted the truth." He continued to tease her as if she'd been pressing him to recount the incident, instead of doing her best to ignore him. "It was raining. And I came back late from fixing an engine. The dinner you'd cooked was ruined."

"You had grease all over your face," she muttered, her tone softening, the words coming as if she couldn't stop them.

"You wouldn't let me inside."

"You were filthy."

Even ten years later, he could hear the same objection in her tone now as she'd had then. And until just this moment, he hadn't realized how much he missed their arguments. He'd missed the sound of her voice, missed her sharp wit and intensity. Odd how he could be this melancholy over the bad times as well as the good ones.

"You made me take off my clothes and then sprayed me down with a garden hose." He couldn't quite summon any outrage. Not with the memories of what they'd shared returning with a depth that made him wistful.

"That's not all I did."

He chuckled. "You were like a lioness, keeping a dirty cub from entering her lair."

"Back then I did whatever the hell I wanted. I didn't think about the neighbors peeping through the rain or the bushes. I could only think about you."

Travis grinned wider. "We were idiots."

"We were in love." She shook her head. "Well, I was in love. You were in lust."

He didn't deny it. "I didn't know what love was back then." And he still didn't. He appreciated that she hadn't pointed out the obvious. Oh, Travis loved his sister. For Ellie, he would give his life. But in his book, love for a sibling was obligatory, nothing like loving a woman like Sandy. Actually, he might not have it in him. He'd given their old relationship his all, and it hadn't been enough. Travis didn't like failure.

He'd found few things in life off-limits. But finding the right woman to fit his lifestyle seemed to be one of them. Perhaps he was too much a loner. Maybe he was too selfish. Perhaps he'd just never met the right woman. Or hadn't stayed in one place long enough to give love a chance to blossom. But Sandy had claimed it was his ego, and his need to be right all the time, that held him back.

Maybe she was correct. He sure didn't know why he'd never connected with another woman the way he had with Sandy Vale. Perhaps it had been fear of failing again. Perhaps he feared the pain of losing someone he cared about. Perhaps drifting through his life was the easiest course of action. Or perhaps his memories of what had passed between them were colored by the lust of youth. He'd almost convinced himself that the sex between them couldn't possibly have been as good as he remembered—until he recalled Sandy's kiss when she'd first greeted him.

It had shot all his nerves into firing at full cadence. And they had yet to settle down. Talking and arguing with her didn't seem to stop him from wanting her every time he looked at her. Between the restless strands of blond hair that escaped her practical ponytail and framed her face, to her eyes the color of a stormy north sea, to her sassy retorts, she was the most attractive woman he'd ever known. Sure, he'd been with some world-class beauties, but none could match Sandy's spunk, her inner beauty that shone through her lightly tanned skin like twenty-four-carat gold.

Sandy's loyalty to Ellie, their close friendship

through the years and her determination to mortgage the only home she'd ever had to save her friend, were qualities rare as a flawless diamond, but even more precious. Travis had found that kind of loyalty among the men of the Shey Group. He knew those same character traits existed in women, but to find it within the only woman who'd ever loved him seemed somehow suspect. And he wondered if his work had made him more cynical and jaded than he'd realized, because in his heart, in the deepest recesses of his brain and in every cell of his body, he knew Sandy was just what she appeared—loyal to the bone.

"Ever wonder how our lives would have changed if I'd been pregnant?" Sandy murmured, clearly lost in thoughts of the past, like he was.

Despite their lust, they'd been responsible about birth control. Yet, he recalled the time she'd been late as if it were yesterday—the metallic taste of fear in his dry mouth, his heart pounding his ribs, how they'd bought the pregnancy kit together. He'd been determined to do the right thing, and had insisted that they would marry if the test turned out positive. All the same, he'd been frightened that he might become a father before he'd had a chance to become a man.

"We would have married. I wouldn't have left you."

"We weren't ready to be parents. We wouldn't have made it. I've never once regretted that the test turned out negative," she told him, yet he heard a hitch in her throat that she cleared with a determination that didn't surprise him at all. "We weren't ready to be parents, emotionally or financially. Sheesh. I could barely take care of myself."

"Yeah. You didn't even have the sense to come in out of the rain." Travis deliberately lightened the moment by teasing her about their wild lovemaking. After she'd washed the grease off him with the garden hose, the heavens had rained down, soaking her. Unwilling to ruin her wood floors, she'd stripped until she was as naked as he'd been. They'd made love up against the side of her house, rain cascading over them, with only the heat of their tangled bodies to keep them warm.

"We were lucky we weren't arrested." She lifted her chin and laughed.

"Or that Ellie didn't come home ten minutes sooner." His sister had returned early, and all bummed out from a sailing race that had been canceled due to the storm. Funny the way his thoughts always circled back to Ellie. Maybe that's why he'd never forgotten Sandy through the years apart. To him, the three were like corners of the same eternal triangle. And someday, if Ellie ever settled down, he wanted her husband to be the brother Travis had never had.

Meanwhile, it was Travis's job to keep his sister safe. To protect her. But first he had to find her.

ELLIE UNDERSTOOD THAT Alan had protected her from real harm when he'd made that horrible videotape. However, she didn't understand why he had gone out of his way to help her. Since that incident, he'd avoided speaking to her. In fact, he often brought the Frenchman with him when he brought her food, as if there was safety in numbers.

But safety for whom?

Had Alan's help placed him in danger? Ever mindful that her cell might be bugged, she went out of her way to remember that speaking to him or revealing that he might be her ally might betray him. Once, when he'd been slightly behind the Frenchman, he nodded to her, his eyes flashing respect. Of course, it might have been her imagination, or a trick of the light.

Alan left her food and another magazine. But most of all, he gave her hope.

She didn't believe it a coincidence that, as he departed from her cell, she heard him speaking to the Frenchman about the sailboat Sandy was supposed to bring to the island in exchange for Ellie.

"They found the boat," Alan told the Frenchman.

"C'est bon."

It is good, Ellie translated, her limited high-school French actually up to the task of following the conversation.

"The hull is damaged. Repairing and sailing her is going to take time, but Vanderpelt is not a patient man."

Oh, God.

Was Alan telling her to be patient, too? Knowing that the boat had been found, and that the repairs would soon be under way, gave her hope of rescue. But if Vanderpelt's patience ran out before Sandy could get here, what would happen to Ellie?

Was this Alan's way of telling her that she needed to

try and escape on her own? But how? She'd examined the four rock walls, the concrete floor, the ceiling she couldn't reach even when she stood on the mattress. The place was a fortress. Without tools, there was no way to dig through rock and concrete.

So was it time to think about overpowering her guard? Ellie thought, maybe, yes. When Sandy finally arrived, Ellie needed to be ready to escape. Because no matter how happy Vanderpelt was to get his damn boat, he couldn't simply release Ellie without facing legal consequences. Kidnapping was not acceptable—and she doubted he would let her live long enough to go to the authorities.

Ellie methodically chewed and swallowed her food. Then did two hours' worth of exercises. She needed to remain strong. She needed a plan. And she wondered if she might get Alan to help her again, because most of all, she really needed a weapon.

And right now, she couldn't even ask for help. Not with the likelihood of a hidden camera focused on her 24/7. Not with the cell bugged to pick up her every word.

Think. She couldn't speak or pantomime her needs. If she only had a pen, she could wait until dark and write a note, find a way to slip Alan a message.

And if she failed? She couldn't be much worse off than she was right now.

TRAVIS AND ELLIE CROSSED the border into Canada on a private charter plane. Kincaid had made all the arrangements, and Ellie realized he'd saved them hours of time.

No rental car companies serviced the small airport, yet Kincaid had a late-model four-wheel drive SUV ready for them, and a private owner had agreed to pilot them wherever they needed to go by boat.

At low tide, the sandbar had left the hull high but not dry. With a huge gash in the bow, she'd taken on water. Beer bottles sloshed in the cockpit and cabin, suggesting someone had stolen the boat and taken a joyride. Either the thieves had abandoned the boat before crashing into rocks, or through incompetence or drunkenness, they'd damaged her during their voyage. Either way, she needed an extensive overhaul.

Ellie shook her head, discouraged at the sad sight. "Getting her off the sandbar is going to be a major headache."

"Not if we patch the hull. Then we'll tow her to a marina, lift her onto a truck and haul her to the manufacturer."

"Sounds like a plan, but we'll never refit her in time."

"*We* can't. But Kincaid can. All we have to do is order supplies for the trip and be ready to go."

"That has to be the understatement of the century." Sandy knew boats. It would take a manufacturer months to make this hull seaworthy. However, they didn't have months, but less than a week.

The pilot cut the engine, and they jumped from the bow of the motorboat onto the sandbar. The pilot handed Travis tools, equipment and a cooler. "When do you want me to return?" he asked in a crusty Canadian accent.

Travis glanced at the current, and Sandy knew he was estimating how long until the tide turned and swept back in. "Three hours?"

"See you then." The taciturn pilot set out a fishing pole and headed upriver at trolling speed, leaving Travis and Sandy alone.

As the boat puttered around a bend, the wind died and the sun seemed to brighten as if mocking them. They stood on a sandbar surprisingly free of shells, at the mouth of an inlet about a hundred miles north of the U.S./Canada border. Sandy had anchored in isolated spots like this one many times, enjoying the tranquility. With the powerboat gone, there were no engine noises, no sounds of people, no airplanes, cell phones or car horns. Just the swish of the gentle breeze, cawing seagulls and lapping water along the sandbar, and the occasional splashing of a fish landing after a leap.

Travis grabbed the toolbox and the bag of gear, and strode to the boat. She dragged the cooler to higher ground, and followed. They'd lucked out in one respect—with the boat lying on its side, the hole in the hull faced the sky, giving them dry access. If she'd been turned the other way, repairs would have been even more difficult.

Although the tide had receded, water remained inside the boat, and would certainly slow towing her and put unnecessary pressure on the already damaged hull. While Travis took out a saw and began to cut away the damaged fiberglass, she removed the plug, allowing some water to drain out of the bilge. Holding the plug, she walked around the keel, examining the damage. The cracks appeared mostly in the fiberglass's outer gel. And the hull, although scraped and bashed, appeared to have only two holes, the major one in the bow and a minor one near the waterline.

After the water stopped draining, she replaced the plug and joined Travis. He'd already removed his shirt, and his muscles clenched as he sawed away the last of the debris. Already tan, his skin glistened with a light sheen of sweat that emphasized his broad chest and lean musculature. Travis wasn't brawny, like a weight lifter, but had the long, lean muscles of a track star. He had large, strong hands, with tapered fingers that clasped the saw with strength and skill. He knew exactly what he wanted to cut, and sliced with an even precision and concentration on his task that allowed her to stare as long as she liked.

And Sandy liked everything about Travis's body. Merle had been correct when she'd said he was perfect to look at. But it wasn't just his great shoulders and chest, or his flat stomach that narrowed into low-rise jeans, that caught her interest.

Sandy appreciated Travis's skill with engines. He had an intuitive know-how for timing and tuning that made his engines purr like a well-satisfied woman. She'd always enjoyed watching him work, finding his expertise sexy. However, reconstruction work was totally different from tuning an engine. As he sawed, tiny particles that looked like sawdust, but were really hardened fiberglass, flew in all directions. From experience, she knew that the material made the skin itch like crazy. Patching the hull wouldn't take long, but from the get-go, it was a dirty, smelly, sweaty job.

Travis didn't complain. Nor did he ask her to take a turn at the saw. Making herself useful, she dug into the bag of gear—once again appreciating Kincaid's practical nature—before setting out the new fiberglass, resin and the hardener that was a chemical catalyst to make the patch dry quickly. "Is your boss a sailor?"

"I have no idea."

"Then how does he always know what we'll need?" she asked, curious about the Shey Group. So far, she was very impressed. From the smooth arrangement of transportation in the wilds of Canada, to the specialized equipment to patch a hull, Kincaid had proven a flair for anticipating their needs.

Travis grinned, but didn't stop sawing. "He's a man who always consults experts. If we had a mission to Alaska, he'd ask the Inuit, as well as the marines, what gear would be required. Then he'd consult survival experts and medical people and weather experts, and boil the information down before coming up with the right stuff.

"There's a med kit in the gear bag."

"And probably a hunting knife, a GPS, a satellite phone, matches, batteries and a flashlight, as well as fishing hooks and mosquito repellent just in case we get stuck out here."

She craned her neck in the direction their ride had disappeared to. "Is that likely?"

"Kincaid prepares for the worst possibility, but I'm sure he also checked out not only our pilot's background but the reliability of his boat before he hired him."

"I can see how it would be a pleasure to work for a man like him."

"Yeah. His men would follow him into hell, if he asked." Travis finished sawing and grabbed a screwdriver to open the can of resin. Then he carefully cut several swatches of fiberglass matting that he would crisscross over the hole. The trick was mixing the correct amount of hardener with the resin. Too little, and the patch would take too long to dry. Too much, and the chemical catalyst would fire before they had the patch in place.

Travis didn't read the directions on the side of the can. He seemed to mix the ingredients by instinct, or smell. The reeking artificial odor was unpleasant, especially from their position downwind. But moving along the hull wasn't an option.

After donning gloves, Travis laid strips of woven fiberglass over the opening, then painted the hardening mixture over the edges. "It won't be pretty, but it should hold until we tow her back to the marina."

Carefully, he built up the layers. And then he moved on, repeating his task at the second hole. The sticky, smelly process was done, but their clothes and hair and skin smelled. Sandy longed to swim, and she imagined that Travis felt much worse since he had the fiberglass dust sticking to his skin. So she wasn't surprised when he shucked the gloves and peered at the incoming tide.

Their task had taken thirty minutes, leaving the hull's patch with plenty of time to harden before the rising water floated the boat.

"How about a swim?"

"Kincaid didn't pack swimsuits, did he?" she responded evenly, but her pulse kicked up a notch.

As if reading her reaction, Travis chuckled and unbuttoned his jeans. "Kincaid isn't the kind of man to consider swimsuits necessary equipment." Travis paused before he slid the jeans off his hips, his eyes sparkling with challenge. "You going to watch? Or join me?"

Chapter Seven

Travis had no idea if she'd watch or join him. One thing he knew for certain, she wouldn't turn her back and pretend nudity offended her. Sandy didn't play those kinds of head games. She might scream and shout at him, she might even hold a grudge, but she enjoyed looking at him as much as he adored looking at her. Although he'd been busy sawing, he hadn't been immune to her appreciative glances while he'd been working. And he figured the cold water would serve two purposes: give them time to consider their next step, and cool their raging hormones.

Shucking his jeans, he tossed them over the dry stern. When her gaze followed his every step, settling on his bare back and butt while her lips pursed in an aggravated pout, he barely contained a grin. "You coming?"

She shooed him into the water with a hand gesture. "You go ahead."

So she planned to watch from a safe distance. Maybe that was best. The old Sandy wouldn't have hesitated. But then, the old Sandy had tended to be wild and reckless, as well as willful and bratty. Now he should be glad that a saner head prevailed. But he wasn't glad. Deep down, he wanted her to join him and acknowledge that she wanted him as much as he wanted her.

Maybe a hot fling would burn her out of his system. Then he reminded himself that that hadn't worked years ago, and probably wouldn't now. Obviously their passion had never burned low. But passion wasn't enough to keep them together—that took something they just didn't have.

Travis stood on the beach, his toes just inches from the lapping water. He might not have taken a summer swim this far north in the Atlantic Ocean in years, but he recalled there was only one way to enter the water—at a full run. Anything less would allow the icy temperatures to stop the process of full immersion.

With a lunge, he sprinted until the water reached his thighs. Then he dived forward headfirst, bracing against the shocking cold that clutched his chest so tightly, he couldn't draw breath for a moment. Then his body adjusted, and he swam out in fierce strokes to increase his circulation, letting the washing action of the waves carry away the itchy fiberglass particles and soothe his skin.

A strong freestyle swimmer, he breathed every three strokes, first to the right and then to the left, grabbing air in the pocket under one arm then the other as he surged forward, his legs kicking and propelling him with the efficiency of a Navy SEAL. As he turned his head to breathe, a shout of pure joy jolted him out of his rhythm.

Stopping to tread water and look behind him, he wasn't exactly surprised to spy Sandy's abandoned clothes tossed next to his, or her steady strokes as she followed him. The little minx. He would have enjoyed watching her disrobe. Would have enjoyed seeing her plunge into the water. But he didn't allow those thoughts to stop his anticipation of her joining him. Where they went from here would be up to her.

Despite the frigid water temperature, he still felt a tingling zip of interest down south. Reminding himself that just because she'd decided to swim with him didn't mean she wanted more failed to stop his heartbeat from skittering. The sexual attraction between them had always been inexplicably, passionately overwhelming, and defied common sense or good reason. Repeating the same errors he'd made in the past would be insane. Even now, as he considered the possibility of having her again, he knew it would be a mistake.

She didn't stop swimming until they were mere inches apart, treading water. Although the pleasant arch of her breasts intrigued him, it was her expression that captivated him. Her eyes reflected the green of the sea, and sparkled like rare emeralds set in gold. Her wet hair, slicked against her head, emphasized her high cheekbones and an elegant facial structure. But it was the pulse in her neck that clued him in that she still reacted to him in a way she couldn't contain.

Bobbing in the water, she came within an inch of his lips, and her voice was a husky murmur. "We shouldn't do this."

"Absolutely not." He swam a little closer, until her breath fanned his lips.

"We aren't right for one another," she told him, her lips brushing his.

"I agree."

Her scent, a mixture of citrus and spice, teased his nostrils, inflaming his senses. He'd never wanted to kiss a woman so badly in his life. He'd never felt such unquenchable hunger, such a driving desire. But he was determined to let her not only come to him, but to make the first move.

"We'll only end up arguing." She peered into his face, her expression intense as she traced her hand along his shoulder, as if unable to refrain from touching him. The old sizzle seemed renewed, more exciting, more dangerous.

"Maybe we shouldn't talk. Maybe you should just shut up and kiss me," he teased, recalling just how easily he could push her buttons, and how much she enjoyed the give-and-take. "After all, kissing me again will probably be the biggest mistake of your life."

"Uh-huh."

And pushing her emotional buttons was not all that he recalled that she liked. Would she still enjoy his attention to her exquisite breasts? Still go wild when he nipped the sensitive spot under her jaw? "Kissing me will lead to…other things."

She raised an eyebrow. "It's not like you to be so vague."

"You want me to elaborate?"

"Yes, please."

"If you kiss me," he said, frowning at her, "I'd have to kiss you back."

"I see." She barely restrained a full smile, but one corner of her mouth turned up.

"And if you kissed me back, then I'd have to discover if one kiss would satisfy you." He let her see the questions in his eyes. If they started making out, he wasn't sure he'd be able to stop short of taking her completely.

"I don't believe one kiss would be enough to satisfy me. Not even *you* are *that* good a kisser."

"Are you complimenting, or complaining?" he teased, knowing full well she wanted to incite him into kissing her first.

"I can't think," she admitted with a shiver. "This water is so cold, my flesh is going numb."

He peered at her. "And your lips are turning blue. Perhaps we should swim to shore, and then I'll let you warm me up."

"You'll let me?" She sprayed him with water from an open palm slap to the surface, then swam back to the beach.

He trailed behind her, wondering if he should have taken that kiss, wondering if once she reached land, she would change her mind. The new Sandy was unpredictable, complex and fascinating.

And he simply cared for her too much to casually make love to her and then move on again. He really needed to stop, think and analyze. He needed to figure out what the hell he wanted and what he was doing.

Yet the moment they both placed their feet on the sand and ran ashore hand in hand, he didn't know if he could resist her. Especially when she flung her arms around him, pressed her wet breasts with her hard nipples against him, tipped backed her head and demanded, "Kiss me, Travis."

Maybe a stronger man could have foregone the temptation. Maybe a better man would have done the noble thing. Maybe some knight in shining armor would have found the willpower to walk away. He couldn't.

Travis simply angled his head, slanted his lips over hers and took what she offered.

SANDY WANTED HIM.

While she should have been wiser now, more careful, more sane, she was simply tired of fighting herself. Flinging her arms around him, lifting her mouth to Travis for a kiss, seemed simple. And right.

Smooth and hard, his skin stretched firmly over sinewy, long muscles, and was as different from hers as canvas from silk. Yet the rough texture of his bronzed flesh pleased her as much as his clean scent of salt and sea and sunshine. Pleased her as much as his raspy breath against her lips. Pleased her as much as his hesitation that told her he was assuming nothing, not taking her for granted in any way.

Damn the consequences. For too long she'd tried to be practical, to protect herself from hurt. And she was wound up as tight as a rubber ball, with no place to bounce. She needed him naked in her arms like this. She tried to forget the past and the future. There was only now, and she wanted to live in the moment.

With his eyes going smoky and his lips tempting her, she lifted up on her toes to have more of him. "God, I've missed...us."

"Me, too." He nibbled a path along her jawline.

She trembled in anticipation, her fingers tightening and drawing him closer. "How do you do this to me?"

He kissed her forehead, her nose, her lips. "What?"

"Make me want you."

He moaned an answer into her mouth. Words that she didn't understand, yet she no longer had need for words. Not with his tongue dancing with hers, both of them flowing in step to a beat only they could hear. She wished they had more time and, contradictorily, wished he'd hurry.

Easy.

Slow down and enjoy him.

Focus on every sound and scent and feeling, to remember him always.

Past mistakes had taught her to savor the intense earthiness of Travis. His powerful body, so different from hers, seemed the perfect complement. Hard and soft. Intense and mellow. Blazing need and ripping desire.

Travis was the only man she'd ever met who could make her simmer with desire and explode into mind-numbing passion. Chemistry, some people called it. She had long since given up trying to classify or name exactly what drove her into his arms with all the explosive force of a full-blown spinnaker. She only knew that the elements driving them together were as mighty as a hurricane and as dynamic as a sea spout.

Kissing Travis was like running wildly downwind and surfing mountain-sized waves at three knots over hull speed. Resisting him was as ludicrous as swimming against a riptide. Their actions might lead to instability and eventual heartache, but just as the wind and water eventually collide, she and Travis came together as if fate had given them no other option.

Breathless, she pulled back to see the storm of need brewing in his eyes—twin thunderclouds of pure passion jolted her with spiraling energy. The froth of her hair skimmed his chest, and his nipple puckered. Dipping her head, she caught the tiny bud between her teeth and teased the tip with her tongue, keeping him exactly where she wanted him. Her fingers skimmed up the insides of his thighs, grazing lightly.

Then his hands combed into her hair, his fingers clenching just hard enough to let her know that his patience had about run out. With a grin, she lifted her eyes to his. "See something you want?"

"I see lots that I want." And with a move that surprised her, he scooped her into his arms and carried her up the beach, back to where they'd left the gear.

She leaned back into him and enjoyed the play of sunlight over his chest, the shadow of arm and shoulder muscles barely tensing as if she were weightless. "Where are you carrying me?"

"Kincaid packed a thermal blanket."

"And condoms?"

"Standard equipment."

He set her down, and she immediately dug into the pack for the blanket. Thin, insulated and waterproof, shiny on one side to reflect the sun, the blanket would protect them from the sand. She leaned over on hands and knees to spread out the corners while Travis dug into the pack, grunting as he searched. He came up with the condoms just as she was about to turn toward him.

"Don't move."

"Excuse me?" She didn't move though, excitement shimmying through her.

"I want to take you like that."

Before she could utter a word, he dropped to his knees behind her, then sat back on his heels, pulling her into his lap. When his hands cupped her breasts, she leaned her head back against his shoulder and sighed. "I didn't know how much I missed you until now."

"Is this all you missed about me?" He tweaked her nipples, then ran his thumbs over them in smooth sensual circles that made holding still close to impossible, because he felt so good.

"Actually, there's another part of you, poking my backside, that I've missed."

He caressed her in the sunlight, the waves gently

lapping the beach, and she should have been at peace. But with the simmering tension he stoked, she just barely refrained from squirming. However, she couldn't prevent the quivers of excitement, or the trembling heat coursing through her like a torrential rain.

She wanted him inside her, and she wanted him now. While she had no doubts that if she remained still, he would continue to caress her until she melted, she couldn't wait. Her need pumped with hot demands.

Lifting her hips and spreading her thighs, she took him inside her while he continued to stroke her breasts. It took only moments to find her rhythm. But then his hand dropped to her parted thighs, slipped into the heat of her folds.

"Slow down," he murmured in her ears.

"Can't."

"Babe, there's no rush."

"Ah. You…may…not be. I am." Her breaths came in gulping gasps. She could barely hold on. Her senses spun and his clever fingers kept up a tempo that drove her wild.

She didn't know exactly when he'd shifted her to her hands and knees and took total control. She only knew that the feel of him sliding in and out of her was incredible, erotic and special. She used her muscles to clench him. Once. Twice.

"You…don't…play…fair," he rasped between thrusts.

"I can't hold…back," she muttered.

"So don't."

She climaxed then, her muscles greedily spasming in a bubbling bliss. But Travis never stopped moving, his fingers never stopped teasing her, and she discovered her body wasn't done. He was taking her up again, to a place she'd never explored. Only she hadn't yet recovered from her previous meltdown, and she was so sensitive, she almost screamed with the pleasure he was giving her.

She clawed at the blanket, her hips gyrating, her senses spinning. And this time when she exploded, she took him over the edge with her. Stars went off like bottle rockets in her head. She wasn't sure if she had screamed his name, but it didn't matter—his name was branded in her mind for all time.

When she could think again, she found herself lying on her side, with him spooning her and still inside her. His hand gently caressed her cheek and his heart pounded as he nestled against her back. "You are incredible."

"And you are terrible," she teased, craning her neck to look at him. Face flushed and tanned, eyes merry and bright, he looked so satisfied, she couldn't resist joking. "I could have had a heart attack."

"Yeah, but I would have been worth it." He grinned, cocky as hell, and she wondered what she was going to do about him.

As if reading her mind, he held her tightly. "Don't think. Not yet."

Easy for him to say. She couldn't turn off her thoughts like a spigot. Her mind wasn't that disciplined. However, with her body so content, it was hard to drum up any angst about the future.

Until a phone rang.

Travis sighed, kissed her ear and stood as it rang again. "Sorry. I have to answer that."

"I thought we weren't doing phone calls."

"Kincaid sent a satellite phone with full encryption. If someone's listening, and if they are really good, they might trace the call but they won't be able to decipher the code." He fumbled through the duffel as the phone rang a third time. "And Kincaid wouldn't call unless it's important."

On the fourth ring, he plucked out the phone and pressed the speaker option so she could hear everything. Standing nude on the beach with the phone to his ear, he looked like some kind of ancient warrior using the latest in modern technology.

"Yes?"

"Four rings to answer the phone. Are you under fire?"

Travis shot her a grin. "My hands were occupied, and she's listening."

"Good." Kincaid surprised her when he approved. She'd expected him to tell Travis to keep the call private. Obviously, she shouldn't have been surprised at his appearances—after all, he was the one who always included condoms in those packs. "We have a situation."

Kincaid's tone hadn't changed, but Travis was already reaching into the pack. His hand came out with a weapon. "I'm listening."

"Vanderpelt's hired another sailing crew to bring him a Canadian boat into the United States."

"To his island?" Travis asked.

"This time the destination is farther south, to a small town called Lighthouse Red on the coast of Maine."

"I wouldn't call Lighthouse Red a town," Sandy contributed. "Maybe a dozen people live there."

"We think he may be trying to smuggle something into the United States. A lead keel is the perfect place to hide an illegal cargo. But he's got guards around the boat. We can't get near it without tipping him off. However, I can use a diversion to get you two on as crew."

"But we have to fix this boat and go after Ellie," Sandy protested.

"We still aren't sure Ellie is on Vanderpelt's island. Maybe she's being held hostage in Lighthouse Red. If you decide to replace the Canadian crew, I can get this boat ready for you in the meantime.

"We'll move the boat to a fenced yard. Use body doubles. We can pull this off, but there's another problem."

"What?" Travis's tone was terse.

"Expert meteorologists don't like the weather patterns. That area of the ocean could be in for some major storms. We're looking at a sixty percent chance of gale-force winds and a ninety percent chance of storm warnings along the entire northeastern seaboard. Decide, and get back to me ASAP."

Kincaid cut the connection, obviously unwilling to extend the conversation longer than necessary. They'd always suspected that Vanderpelt might not have kept Ellie on his island. Now they had another place to search. But if they chose wrong, would they have enough time to sail this boat to Vanderpelt? Especially with the storm coming in?

This was one decision Sandy didn't want to make. It was like betting on a poker hand when one couldn't see the cards—with the stakes being Ellie's life.

Travis set down the phone and the gun, and strode nude to the water. She stood and joined him, knowing this had to be his decision, but wanting to give him support. When she came up beside him, Travis took her hand but didn't say anything. They waded into the water, washed, then returned to shore.

After sharing a chamois to dry off, they dressed and repacked the gear. She noticed he left the phone and gun on top. Then they checked the hull patches. Travis had done a fine job. The fiberglass had hardened. When the tide floated the hull, she could now be towed to a boatyard and refitted. Sandy stared at the keel, realizing the lead could hide a multitude of objects. Diamonds. Heroin. Bioterrorism materials. Anything.

If they melted the lead to find out what was inside, they might destroy the cargo, but they might also destroy the chance to rescue Ellie. Better to deliver the boat, get Ellie back, then make a move on Vanderpelt. That much was obvious. But should she and Travis try to sail the second boat to Lighthouse Red? Could Ellie be there? Or was it a wild-goose chase? And if not, would the weather allow them time to make two voyages?

Although a million questions hammered at her, she didn't want to press Travis, didn't want to influence his decision. While Sandy was sure she loved Ellie every bit as much as he did, Ellie was his sister. His blood. His only living relative. After their parents died, he'd raised Ellie, and the connection remained strong. Sandy had no right to call the shots. No right to an opinion. However hard it was for her to remain silent, the choice had to be his.

Travis set two anchors to prevent the boat from floating higher on the sandbar as the tide rushed in. He worked quickly, tying off the lines to the cleats, digging the anchors deep into the sand to prevent slippage. And then he walked along the beach, picking up flat stones and tossing them into the sea, skipping them across the calm surface.

His actions might have seemed controlled, but she sensed the bubbling frustration underneath. She'd never done anything as hard as waiting silently for him to make a decision. And she tried not to think what she would do if the decision was hers. That was impossible, of course.

Sandy wanted to see to the refitting of the boat herself. The hull was a wreck. If they were going to face a giant storm, she wanted to oversee the repairs, especially the setting of the mast. If they capsized at sea and went down, they couldn't help Ellie. Although Sandy had respect for Kincaid's ability, sailing was her area of expertise. And she believed in her heart that Ellie was on Vanderpelt's island—not at a second location.

"Well?" Travis finally said something.

With the sound of their ride chugging around the bend, they didn't have time for a long conversation. Yet, as they dressed, they spoke quietly.

"It's your decision," she told him.

"You have an opinion?"

"I have a preference, based on nothing but intuition. It's your call."

"And what does your intuition say?"

She hadn't wanted to say. But he'd asked, so she gave her opinion. "I think she's with Vanderpelt on his island."

"Because of the phone calls?"

"No."

"Then why?" Travis grabbed her shoulders and spun her to face him. "What aren't you telling me?"

She breathed in and let out a sigh. "When we sailed away, I didn't like the way Vanderpelt looked at Ellie's legs."

"What?"

"It could have been nothing. Men always look at Ellie." Exasperation with him entered her tone, despite her best efforts to remain calm.

"But?"

"I just had the feeling that he was interested in her…like a man is interested in a woman."

"Damn it. You should have told me."

"Why? So you could worry more? We're already doing everything we can. And I could have been wrong. The glint in Vanderpelt's eyes could have been a simple trick of the light. I don't think my impression should influence your decision."

"Kincaid believes we have time to sail to Lighthouse Red and, if it turns up zip, still make the island, or he wouldn't have suggested it."

At the agony in Travis's eyes, her heart sank. No one should have to make such a choice. "So does that mean you've made a decision?"

Chapter Eight

"Yes." Travis's positive tone irritated her, especially since the confidence in his voice contrasted with the indecision she'd read in his eyes. "We're going to let Kincaid refit this hull while we check out Lighthouse Red."

"What about the brewing storm?" she asked, arguing, even though she'd told herself she wouldn't do this, but unable to stop herself…as usual.

"We have to refit this boat. It's not as though we could beat the weather and sail to the island now. While we're waiting, we might as well check out the other location." His mind made up, he didn't want to consider her point of view, and that irritated her almost as much as his determination. "Besides, the storm might not happen. Meteorology isn't an exact science."

"Yeah, the storm could arrive early. Weather might delay us at Lighthouse Red. Or worse, Ellie might not be there, and one of Vanderpelt's men might recognize me from my time on the island."

"It's a chance we'll have to take."

"Travis, you're gambling with Ellie's life," she practically shouted at him. The man was so damn stubborn. She didn't believe he'd considered all the options, or he wouldn't be so willing to take such unacceptable risks. The cessation of phone calls from Alan to Vanderpelt indicated that they were in close enough proximity not to need phone communication. And Ellie had last been seen with Alan. It made sense that she was there, not at Lighthouse Red.

"Either choice is a gamble. I'm hoping to cover both alternatives."

"Look, if we're supposed to deliver the boat to Vanderpelt in exchange for Ellie, he'd expect us to ask to see her before sailing up to his dock, wouldn't he? So he'd keep her close by to use her to get what he wants."

"Not necessarily." Travis shook his head, his tone firm and louder than normal. "If he said no to our request to see Ellie, we'd have to dock the boat anyway."

While they weren't quite yelling at one another, they were close to it. His shoulders tensed. A telltale muscle throbbed as he clenched his jaw, and his stiff neck told her he was moments from exploding. She'd anticipated this argument, told herself to let him decide—and yet, she cared too damn much to remain silent. Reminding herself that he was equally upset hadn't changed anything.

But she could do something now that she hadn't been able to do years ago—she could also see his side. She thought he was wrong, but she understood how he could opt to check out both scenarios. So she walked to him, placed her hands around his waist and laid her cheek against the stiff muscles of his back. "Whatever we do, we're going together."

He turned within the circle of her arms. "Thank you."

Was she dreaming? She'd expected him to kick sand, throw more rocks and release several curses. She wouldn't have been surprised if he'd jerked away and stalked down the beach to meet their ride. But now he was staring down at her with a searching intensity, almost tenderness, as if he'd never seen her before. And he'd thanked her. "I'm so worried about Ellie, I'm not sure I'm thinking straight. It must be even more difficult for you. I wasn't trying to give you a hard time. I just wanted to make sure you'd considered all the alternatives."

"That's why I was thanking you. I understand that." He snorted. "Once, I would have thought you just wanted to prove a point."

"And once…you might have been right." She swallowed a lump in her throat. "But saving Ellie is too important for there to be anything but honesty between us. I don't want to fight with you. I want her back home, safe."

"Me, too."

Travis kissed Sandy. And he'd never kissed her like this. Usually his kisses sizzled right down to her toes. But this kiss was tender, warming her heart and making her realize that while she'd always admitted that she cared about Ellie, she'd never admitted that to herself about Travis. When she thought of him, she thought of hot sex, irresistible chemistry and huge fights that left her furious. She'd never realized that she cared about him, too.

She hated that the decisions must be tearing him apart. That for all his skills and connections, he still might not be able to save Ellie. The idea of failure sickened her and she swayed into him. Travis's arms tightened. "We're going to get her back."

VANDERPELT WATCHED HIS prisoner through the hidden camera in her cell. His spying gave him not only a sense of power but a secret thrill. He enjoyed watching her pace like a caged animal. He enjoyed watching her slender body stretch and go through her exercise routines. Too bad he hadn't thought to install a shower in her quarters. He would have enjoyed that, too—but not as much as watching her quiet tears.

He hadn't permitted Alan to take her out of her cell. He wanted to be the man to do so. She would be grateful, and he intended to be the recipient of that gratitude. Another day, he decided. One more day of no one to talk to and nothing to do and she would be ready to crack. She'd do anything he asked.

"Sir." Alan poked his head into Vanderpelt's office. "You have a moment?"

Vanderpelt had difficulty keeping the explosive harshness from his voice. "Not if you've come begging at the prisoner's behest."

"No, sir. We've had good news. We've hired a Canadian husband and wife team to deliver the second boat to Lighthouse Red."

"They've done this before?"

Alan nodded. "Should be no problem getting the boat past customs."

"Good."

"And Sandy Vale and Travis Cantrel have found your stolen boat. They are hoping to refit her and sail here before the storm."

"We'll be ready for them."

"And one more thing."

"Sir?"

"Don't bring Ellie any more food."

Vanderpelt wanted her good and hungry when he laid out a tempting lunch for her. He anticipated her sitting on his lap, eating from his fingers in grateful appreciation of his largesse. His mouth salivated in anticipation.

Alan's face didn't change expression. "May I ask why?"

Vanderpelt shook his head, but couldn't restrain a satisfied chuckle. Ah, tomorrow was going to be a reward for a job well-done.

TRAVIS APPRECIATED SANDY'S skill as she steered the boat, luffing the wind from the sails. He eased the anchor down, judging the distance to the bottom and then allowing three times that distance of line for scope. Then he took down the jib while Sandy drew in the mainsail. With the boat shipshape, and within minutes of drawing into a cove ten miles north of the town of Lighthouse Red, he was eager to row the dinghy ashore to the car Kincaid had waiting.

They planned to check out the tiny marina by land before sailing in blindly. One good thing about small towns was that everyone knew everyone else's business. Strangers would stick out like a machine gun in a case of revolvers.

Travis lowered the dinghy from the transom and then rowed ashore. Sandy sat silently, her face tipped to the sun. During the sail down the U.S. coast, they'd taken alternate shifts. One of them slept while the other stayed at the tiller. Although they had self-steering on the boat, they wanted to make the best time, and that took micromanagement of sail adjustments to take advantage of every puff of wind.

They hadn't talked much since their last argument, and for that Travis was grateful. Sandy was risking her life to help him find Ellie. But as often as he'd tried to remind himself that Sandy was entitled to her opinion, once they reached land, he was the expert, and she had to accept his skill just as he did hers while they were at sea.

"So what's the plan?" Sandy asked, her voice level, her gaze avoiding his as she took in the rocky coastline stepped with green fir and pine. "A little to the right," she directed.

With his back to the shore, she had a better view, and he didn't hesitate to follow her directions. He didn't understand why she couldn't be as accommodating when the situation was reversed. Shoving the complaint to the back of his mind, he pulled on the oars, finding the exercise soothing. As for the plan… "We go into town and look around. We'll pretend to be travel writers, so we can ask questions without raising suspicion."

"I'm with you, so far." Sandy raised an eyebrow. "And what are we really after?"

"In a place as tiny as Lighthouse Red, strangers will be noticed. Our story will be about the merits of visiting the place. And who better to ask than out-of-town visitors?"

"So that's why you wanted me to bring pad and paper. To take notes?"

"Yes. But I've been gone for a long time. You know New Englanders better than I do. I want you to look for discrepancies and variations from a pattern."

"Huh?"

"Just watch out for anything that makes you suspicious."

"All strangers seem suspicious to me," she muttered.

"That's the conservative, Yankee, New Englander in you talking."

"A little more to the left," she directed. "Did you just insult me?"

He chuckled. "I was stating facts."

"Yeah, but you made me sound as if my values are conditioned into me instead of chosen."

"Aren't we all a product of our genes and our environment?"

"Our environment is going to be smacking into rocks if you don't pull harder to the left."

"The current is strong here."

She shrugged. "Tide's coming in. We're almost at the full moon."

"You ever been to Lighthouse Red before?" Travis asked.

"Can't say I've had the pleasure. Why?"

"It would be better if none of the locals recognize you."

"It's not the locals I'm worried about, but the people we were supposed to deliver that boat to. If any of Vanderpelt's men saw me on his island and now again here..."

"Kincaid has a disguise for you in the car—a brunette wig, sunglasses, a large straw hat. Strangers won't recognize you."

After they pulled ashore and hid the dinghy amid some brush, they found the vehicle right where Kincaid had promised. She tied up her hair, opened the kit bag and plopped on the wig and hat. After she added the sunglasses, not even Ellie would have recognized her.

The drive into town, along winding switchbacks, took half an hour. They parked along the main road lined, with tourist shops that sold homemade fudge and souvenir T-shirts depicting the red lighthouse for which the town was named, a gourmet grocery, a pharmacy and a barbershop. There were more people strolling along the sidewalks than Travis had anticipated.

While gravitating toward a small marina to the side of a pier that promised whale sightings, Travis picked up a tail following them. The man was oh-so-skilled, and Travis might not have spotted him in a larger town with a greater population. His first instinct was to catch the guy, then beat the hell out of him until the man told him where Ellie was. But Travis no longer followed his first instincts. He'd learned to think, to analyze his position and access all the options. The tail might not be working alone. He could be herding them into an ambush or simply reporting on their movements.

The tail was medium height, medium build, with dark hair and Mediterranean skin. He could be Hispanic, Arabic or Greek. Moving slowly, as if he was out for a stroll, he matched their pace, speeding up when they did, slowing when they did, too.

"Don't turn your head, but we've picked up a tail."

Sandy's voice lowered an octave but she didn't so much as stiffen. "One of Vanderpelt's men? You think someone recognized me with this wig?"

"I don't know. Making assumptions isn't wise. His spycraft is excellent. I almost didn't pick him up. I'd love to know who he works for."

"Why don't we ask him our reporter questions?" she suggested.

Travis kept walking. "But then he would know that we know that he's tailing us."

"You know, it's scary that I actually understood what you just said."

"Very funny." He stopped in the shadow of an ice cream parlor and tugged her into his arms. "Kiss me."

"What?" She stopped and tipped her head up to peer over the sunglasses into his eyes, and he angled his mouth over hers. She didn't object. Didn't push him away. In fact, her arms rose around his neck and pulled him close. Close enough for him to appreciate her breasts against his chest and her citrus scent wafting to him on the breeze. But most importantly, he had a reason to look back the way they'd come.

Their tail appeared to be working alone. Yet, Vanderpelt had instructed the husband and wife crew that Travis and Sandy had replaced to meet *two* men. Hopefully these men wouldn't recognize him, but it was a chance he had to take. If there was another man tailing them, either he was too good for Travis to spot or he was presently out of view.

As much as he enjoyed holding and kissing Sandy, as much as he wanted to think about how he always responded to her kisses—and this time was no exception—he forced his mind to focus on what to do next. Telling himself that if nothing else panned out, he could always confront the tail later, Travis led Sandy onto the pier at a leisurely pace. A vendor hawked his wares—hot pretzels, colas and foot-long hot dogs covered with relishes. Beside him, a woman sold jewelry fashioned from shark teeth. Another artist sold night-lights made from conch shells. Tourists paraded up and down the pier, taking pictures, chasing children and talking loudly, and his plan to question strangers flew by the wayside.

With tourist high season at a peak, almost everyone was from out of town. He needed a new plan, and steered Sandy down a narrow sidewalk toward the town's only marina. "The tourist angle isn't going to work."

"Yeah, I noticed." She checked her watch. "We're supposed to deliver the boat at sunset."

"We aren't going to make it."

"We're not?"

"No. We'll watch from here and see who's waiting for us."

"Sounds like a plan. And then?"

"That depends. Maybe we'll strike up a conversation. Or follow them."

"Why not just invite them for dinner?" she muttered.

He snapped his fingers. "You know, that's not a bad idea. Not if we can think up an angle that will work."

"I was being sarcastic."

"Yeah, I know. But it will be interesting to see, if and when Vanderpelt's guys show up, whether our tail disappears."

"You think Vanderpelt doesn't trust his own men?"

"That's one possibility."

Her eyes narrowed with a measure of disbelief and fear. "What's another?"

"That someone besides Vanderpelt is interested in us and, possibly, our cargo."

"You're scaring me, again."

"I am?"

"Yeah." She bit her bottom lip, her shoulders tense. "It never occurred to me that there could be other players."

SANDY PICKED OUT Vanderpelt's men with as little difficulty as she could have spotted a cinnamon jellybean in a jar full of lemon-yellows. Not only did the men seem uncomfortable walking on the floating dock, their overly-large suit jackets weren't exactly boating attire, nor did their coats hide telltale underarm bulges that indicated they carried weapons.

The leader of the two men had beady eyes set too close together. He looked bulky enough to play nose tackle for the New England Patriots. His cohort was even beefier, and his bald head sweated like a ripe melon in the morning dew.

Sandy plastered on a friendly smile as she and Travis approached the two men, and recalled the names of the Canadian sailors whose jobs Kincaid had arranged for them to take. "Hi, there. I'm Valerie Brooks and this is Dwight Phillips."

Mr. Beady Eyes shook hands, his palm sliding over hers with a slick intimacy that made her want to wipe her palm on her jeans. Sandy pretended the man's stare didn't give her the heebie-jeebies as he spoke in an ordinary voice. "I'm Dan, this is Randall. Where's the boat?"

"I'm afraid we had a little mishap." Travis took over the conversation, drawing the men's attention away from her, which she appreciated.

"What kind of mishap?" Dan practically growled.

"Nothing that can't be overcome by morning." Travis gestured toward a restaurant on the marina property. "I thought we could discuss the voyage over dinner."

"Where's the boat?" Dan asked again, ignoring the invitation.

"I'll show you on a chart...over dinner—which is on me, of course." Travis kept his voice pleasant and light.

Dan and Randall exchanged glances, clearly unsure what to do. If these men were in Vanderpelt's hierarchy, they couldn't be too high up the ladder.

They might not know anything about Ellie's whereabouts. Then again, if they weren't too smart, they might accidentally reveal important details. Sandy hoped they weren't wasting time, but she understood that Travis didn't want to take off for the island without assuring himself that Ellie wasn't still on the mainland.

"You don't get paid until the boat is delivered." Randall spoke for the first time.

"Not a problem." Travis again gestured to the restaurant. "Please, I'm starved and I understand that the lobster here is excellent."

Ten minutes later, they'd settled into a booth and the efficient waitress had taken their orders. After drinks arrived, Travis pulled out a chart. He found the town of Lighthouse Red, then pointed to a bay twenty miles south of where they'd anchored the boat. "We overshot this harbor. With the tide and wind against us, beating into the wind was a chore. We decided to come into town and explain why we were late. We should be able to bring in the boat first thing tomorrow morning."

"Delivery was supposed to be today." Dan munched on oyster crackers.

"We were hoping you wouldn't have to tell your boss." Travis lowered his voice and spoke confidentially. "We'd like to do more work for him."

"There isn't any more work." Randall cracked his knuckles. "And the boss has a schedule to keep."

"Is he planning on taking a cruise?" Sandy asked casually.

Dan almost choked on a cracker. "Yeah, right."

Even she could see the man was lying. But why had he bothered?

"When's your boss coming in?" Travis asked.

"Don't know," Dan muttered.

"Well, if we deliver the boat by noon, and if he doesn't arrive before then, can we keep the navigation error among ourselves?"

Randall shook his head. "The boss doesn't like surprises."

"Then it will be better if he doesn't know what happened," Travis said with deliberate misunderstanding. "Are you two outfitting her for the voyage? Because we could pitch in and help. Save you some time."

Dan frowned at him. "We already have all the supplies we need."

"But we could help stow them and get you squared away," Sandy offered, unsure exactly what Travis was going for, but trying to help.

Dan guffawed. "Do we look like we don't have the muscle to carry a few supplies across the street?"

There was only one hotel across the street. Now that they knew where these men were staying, they could check out the place to see if they had Ellie with them. And after the meal—and as many drinks as Travis could entice the men to consume—they promised to meet at the dock in the morning, but revealed no other pertinent details. Except one.

Randall had given them his cell phone number, so they could call when they got close to Lighthouse Red in the morning. Sandy knew Travis would have the number traced, and have Kincaid do a background check. Perhaps they might turn up even more information.

But first, she sensed that Travis had gone into work mode. She noted his sharpened awareness, an expectancy about him that kept her tense and edgy. As soon as they said goodbye to Dan and Randall, she questioned him. "Is something wrong?"

"We still haven't lost the tail."

"Oh."

"And I don't want to follow Randall and Dan while I'm being watched."

"Can we lose the tail?"

"That would mean we'd have to split up. I'd have to get him to follow me. And I don't want to leave you alone."

She hated being a hindrance. As much as she didn't like the idea of him leaving her, she wanted him free to search the hotel. If there was any chance at all that Ellie might be with Vanderpelt's men, or if he could find a clue to lead them to her, Sandy didn't want to be the reason Travis held back.

"What can I do?" Sandy asked.

"Will you follow my directions, for once in your life?" Travis looked her straight in the eyes, his mouth a firm line of determination.

As her throat closed up with tension, she nodded.

"Walk back into town. Stay in the shops. Don't go anywhere alone. Mix with people." He checked his watch. "Meet me at the kite store in one hour."

"I'll be there," she agreed. As much as she wanted to go with him, she would only slow him down. Whatever he had to do, he needed to be free to do it without worrying about her. Standing on her toes, she leaned into him and kissed his lips. "I'll be fine."

He kissed her slowly, thoroughly, as if they might never do this again. By the time he set her back on her feet, she was breathless, slightly dizzy and warm to the bone. Man, oh man, Travis knew how to kiss. For just a moment, he'd made her forget he was going in alone to face two armed men who outweighed him—and that would be after he lost a very qualified tail.

Meanwhile, she *planned* to do exactly as he'd asked. And Sandy's intentions were the best, right up to the moment a gun pressed into her side and a deadly voice whispered, "Let's go."

Chapter Nine

"Let's go where?" Sandy asked, her heart skittering up her throat.

The man had caught her unawares, about half an hour after she and Travis had separated. She'd been looking at local art, killing time window-shopping and trying hard not to keep glancing over her shoulder for Travis. He'd said he would meet her at the kite store and he would keep his word. She'd have to be patient.

This man wasn't beefy, like Vanderpelt's men. With his average height, weight and skin, he wouldn't be noticed in a crowd. He'd dressed in jeans and a casual, loose, brown jacket. His tone was accented, but she couldn't place it. Not Hispanic, French or English. Not German or Russian.

He nudged her with the gun. "Outside."

Oh, God. Travis had told her to stay inside. With people. But what choice did she have? Making a fuss, when the man could shoot her by just moving his trigger finger, didn't seem a wise move.

She walked out of the store and stopped. She lifted her purse strap off her shoulder. "I don't have much, but if you want money—"

"Let's not play games, Sandra Vale."

Her mouth went so dry, she could barely speak. "You know my name? Do you know Ellie? Do you know where she is?"

"I'm asking the questions. But first, we need to go somewhere more private."

"No." She swallowed her fear. "If you're going to shoot me, do it here."

At least then Travis would find her body and go after her killer.

"I don't work for Vanderpelt and I don't want to hurt you. We need to talk." He took hold of her arm. "Here, I'll put the gun away, and, if you like, we can even wait for Travis to arrive to finish this conversation. Where did he tell you to meet him?"

"Travis?" She tried to play dumb, to stall for time, to think what she should do.

"Travis Cantrel. Big, good-looking American. Your old lover. He's looking for his sister, Ellie."

The man's voice was clipped, efficient, not unfriendly. How did he know so much about them? What was going on? And where was Travis when she needed him?

Sandy didn't know what to do. She didn't want to lead this man to Travis. Obviously, he was dangerous and he might shoot both of them. But she wasn't going to get away from this guy by herself. His grip on her arm was far from painful, but still quite firm. He was alert, wary. And strong.

The compassion in his eyes gave her hope that he wouldn't shoot her, and she considered screaming to draw attention to herself. But suppose the man could help them find Ellie? He obviously knew quite a bit about their situation. She needed more information to make a decision. "I don't believe you told me your name."

"Ari Golden."

"And why were you following me?"

"Because I lost Travis. He's good. So I circled back, figuring he wouldn't leave you alone for long."

Ari Golden was the man who'd been tailing them. While he claimed that he didn't work for Vanderpelt, she didn't quite believe him. And yet, Travis had warned her that there might be other players.

"But why were you following Travis? And who do you work for?"

"First, tell me why you had dinner with Vanderpelt's men."

She saw no reason not to tell him. If Ari worked for Vanderpelt, he already knew they were looking for Ellie. If he didn't, maybe he could help them. "We hoped they might lead us to Ellie."

"And?"

"And what?"

"What else did you learn?"

If Ari had seen them meet Randall and Dan for dinner, and if he worked for Vanderpelt, he might have already reported their blown covers. Randall and Dan could have been expecting Travis to show up. The alarming thought made her ultracautious.

"We didn't learn anything," she lied.

He shot her a skeptical look. "From the drunken condition of those two bozos, I'd say that's highly unlikely."

"But true," she lied again.

He didn't believe her this time, either. "So Travis probably followed them to the hotel to see what else he could learn."

She wasn't surprised Ari had guessed where Travis had gone, and hoped she'd successfully kept her face blank. Meanwhile, she came up with a plan. "Travis is supposed to meet me—" she glanced at her watch "—in a half hour." The time was closer to fifteen minutes, but if Travis showed up early, he might take Ari by surprise. "I'm supposed to meet him outside the ice-cream shop."

Ari gave her a long, hard look that said he didn't believe her but would go along with her shenanigans. But she didn't understand why. She didn't sense evil in him, although his middle name could have been "danger" with a capital *D*. His quiet manner drew no notice, and he blended into the tourist crowd as if he had no private agenda.

She'd picked the ice-cream shop because there they could sit outside at picnic tables, which would give Travis the opportunity to spot her before he arrived at the kite store. Unless he came in from the opposite direction.

Figuring a fifty-fifty chance was better than none, she tried to think ahead. With darkness, the crowds were thinning. Most of the families with children had retired for the night, leaving mostly couples to stroll through the town that was quickly shutting down. All that remained open was the coffee shop, the kite store and the ice-cream parlor.

Sandy had the horrible feeling she shouldn't have said as much as she had. She worried that she should be leading Ari in the opposite direction—but then Travis might never find her. Yet, the thought that she might be placing him in danger by putting herself in a position where he could easily find her also concerned her.

He'd told her to trust him. He'd told her he knew what he was doing. He'd told her he had skills. Well, she hoped that he would be wary. Travis had been away so long, he wasn't familiar with her circle of friends. He might assume Ari was someone she knew, someone who didn't have a gun, someone who wasn't dangerous.

Something about the way Ari moved, with the grace and silence of a panther, reminded her of Travis. The men could have trained in the same military disciplines. For a moment, she wondered if they could both be working for the Shey Group. But Kincaid was never that careless. If Travis's boss had sent a man to watch over them, he would have told Travis.

But if Ari wasn't working for Vanderpelt or the Shey Group, why was he here? She glanced at him with suspicion and fear. Could he know Ellie from somewhere? Or was she way off base?

TRAVIS HAD SLIPPED away from his tail, but it had been more difficult than he'd expected and had taken longer than he would have liked. After he doubled back and sneaked into the hotel room, he found himself thinking more about the tail than about Vanderpelt's snoring drunkards, who didn't so much as turn over when he opened the window and entered their room.

A quick search revealed fake IDs, weapons with serial numbers sanded down and a lot of empty beer cans. He found no receipts in coat pockets or the trash, but made a quick imprint of a credit card—one he suspected might be stolen. Neither of the men carried any personal items. No pictures of family. No health insurance cards.

After carefully taking several empty beer cans that wouldn't be missed—and that might give up fingerprints—Travis exited the hotel as silently as he'd entered. He checked the time. He had enough to spare a stop at a local bar to call Kincaid. The sports bar had televisions tuned to preseason football, golf and tennis. However, one channel reported weather nonstop. Clearly, a storm system was hovering in the Atlantic, and forecasters were predicting a route heading up the northeastern seaboard. However, the storm was currently stalled. If a warm front came up from the south, the storm could peter out. But a cold front out of the east would intensify the disturbance.

Travis waited for the phone to reroute so the encrypted call couldn't be traced. He gave all his information on Dan and Randall to Kincaid, set up a drop box for the beer cans to be checked for prints and listened to progress on the sailboat's refit. Then Kincaid gave him instructions for tomorrow.

Five minutes later, Travis was out the door and heading back into town. Habit made him careful. Although he didn't expect trouble, he approached the kite shop from an alley across the street. Since he'd arrived a few minutes early, he wasn't concerned that Sandy had yet to show up. Five minutes later, his nonchalance changed to real concern, and he slipped deeper into the shadows. Another five minutes, and he cased the street, his tension escalating.

And he found her sitting in front of the ice-cream parlor in earnest conversation with a man he didn't recognize. Damn. Damn. Damn. Had his worry been for no good reason? He should have known better than to get all worked up over her safety. Years ago, Sandy hadn't worn a wristwatch, setting her hours by the sun and the tides. While she now wore a watch, apparently being on time still meant little to her.

At first he assumed she'd met up with someone she knew and forgotten the time. Irritated that she hadn't been worried about him enough to keep their meeting, he almost stalked up to the table.

But then he noted the tense set of Sandy's shoulders, her crossed leg and the foot that kept tapping. Travis took another hard look at her companion and realized his first assumption had been wrong. The man wore a jacket, and the pocket sagged from more than the weight of his hand, as if he carried something heavy. A weapon? The angle was right.

The way he was sitting, Travis couldn't approach without the man seeing him—and he didn't believe the defensive position was a coincidence. His former irritation again spiked into fear for Sandy's safety. She wasn't sitting at that table voluntarily. She hadn't been late to meet him out of carelessness.

Alternatives rushed through his mind. Travis could wait them out, watch to see where they went next. But he feared the stranger might force Sandy into a vehicle, and Travis might lose them.

While he'd left his weapon on the boat, Travis's training made his hands and feet deadly weapons. Hopefully, he could extricate Sandy before violence occurred. He had to weigh the danger to innocent bystanders of gunfire breaking out, but the street was almost deserted. The kid running the ice cream store flicked off the lights and closed up, locking the door and heading off whistling, leaving Sandy and the stranger sitting in the dim light of the street lamps.

That's when Travis stepped from the shadows. The man neither looked surprised to see him approach, nor moved the weapon he probably had trained on Sandy to point at Travis, who was more of a threat. A cool, calculated decision that made Travis more wary. Travis wasn't dealing with street trash. This man knew his business, and the steady look in his eyes, the confident set of his shoulders and his calm expression told Travis that he was a pro.

"We've been expecting you." The man gestured for Travis to take the third chair.

"This is Ari Golden. He's been tailing us," Sandra told him.

Travis took the chair between the two, blocking the man's aim at Sandy. At his smooth move, Ari's eyes narrowed, but the corner of his mouth turned up in an almost appreciative smile.

Travis didn't relax, but he was about to think that they might work things out with conversation when two cars puttered down the street. At the sound of a loud pop, like that of a gun being fired, Travis kicked out the legs of Ari's chair and tackled Sandy to the planked deck.

Ari rolled, coming up with the gun in his hand. In the back of his mind, Travis realized the loud pop had been a car backfiring, not the sound of gunfire. However, with Ari aiming the weapon at them, and with only Travis's body between Sandy and a bullet, Travis wasn't taking any chances. Lashing out with his foot, he kicked Ari's hand, and the gun skidded across the painted deck.

Ari dived on top of Travis and the two men wrestled, rolling over the decking, grunting and cursing as elbows and knees slammed into flesh. Neither man could gain much leverage, and when they struck the curb, they sprang apart and regained their footing.

But not for long.

Ari lunged with a well-aimed right fist to his throat that would have nailed Travis flat, except for a last-second move on his part. As he shifted, he thrust the other man forward, slamming the knife-hand ridge of his fingers between ribs.

Instead of striking a vulnerable organ, his hand met bone. Ari had spun with the force of his blow. He angled his body, blocking, then countering with a foot sweep. Both men, evenly matched in strength and skill, fell hard, rolled and circled one another, looking for a weak area to attack.

This time when Travis heard the gunshot, he froze, fearing that Ari had a partner who'd started shooting. Glancing around, frantic to find Sandy and assure himself she was okay, his gaze settled on her.

She was fine. More than fine. She'd come up with Ari's gun and had fired it. Now, with shaking hands, she pointed it in their direction. "Don't move."

Travis automatically assumed she was talking to Ari, and took a step in her direction. She shook her head. "I said, don't move."

"Uh, in case you haven't noticed, I'm the guy who charged in and risked his neck to save you," Travis muttered, but kept his feet rooted. As badly as her hands were shaking, he didn't trust her not to shoot him by accident.

"You're the guy who acted like a crazy man just because a car backfired," she countered, her tone somewhere between annoyed and scared.

"Ari was holding a gun on you," Travis argued.

"Yeah, but he wasn't going to use it," Ari said, speaking of himself in the third person, as if this was some kind of joke.

"You believe him?" Travis asked Sandy in amazement, wondering what this Ari could have said to her to convince her of his innocence.

"I'd like to." Sandy's eyes focused on the other man. "Ari was about to tell me who he worked for."

"Sorry, ma'am. I can't do that."

"Travis, tell Ari who you work for."

"I can't do that."

She rolled her eyes skyward. "Oh, for heaven's sake. I think we're all on the same damn side."

"Then put down the gun," Ari suggested.

"I'm not an idiot," she snapped.

Travis was about to interfere, but he was enjoying the sight of her holding the gun, enjoying her moment of total control and confidence way too much to speak up just yet.

Ari spoke soothingly. "Nor are you trained to use that weapon, so I suggest—"

"That you answer my question before my untrained self aims and pulls the trigger."

"She just might do it," Travis warned the other man, appreciating Sandy's audacity. "You've made her mad."

"My mother told me not to ever make a beautiful woman mad unless I wanted to hit her or marry her. And hitting a woman is not my style."

Travis grinned. "Sounds like your mother gives good advice."

"Damn it, Travis. This is serious. Tell Ari that you work for the Shey Group."

Travis shook his head and chuckled. "That information is classified."

"You work for Logan Kincaid?" Ari's voice rose an octave in awe. He hadn't flinched at being held at gunpoint. He'd gone hand-to-hand with Travis and had come out even, if breathing a little hard. Nothing had seemed to faze him—until he heard mention of Kincaid.

"Now it's your turn, Mister." Sandy's voice was level, but threaded with steel. "And while you're talking, tell us why you were tailing us."

"Can I make a phone call, first?" Ari asked pleasantly enough.

"And if I say no?" she countered.

"Then you'll have to shoot me." His eyes twinkled. "I need permission to tell you more."

Unsure, she exchanged a look with Travis. He nodded and she answered, "Fine. Move slowly, so you don't scare me. I don't like the sight of blood."

Travis couldn't help it. He chuckled. She might shoot him for laughing, but he just couldn't keep back the belly-rolling laugh at a woman who was holding a gun on two dangerous men, threatening to shoot them and saying she didn't like the sight of blood. Perhaps it was his reaction to finding her safe. All he knew was, once the laughter bubbled up, it took his breath until tears threatened to spill over his cheeks.

Meanwhile, Ari chuckled. Sandy fumed. And Ari called someone and spoke in English so they understood every word. "I believe Travis Cantrel works for the Shey Group. I want permission to share intel." He snapped the phone shut with a satisfied expression. "I'm Mossad."

"Mossad?" Sandy asked.

"Israeli intelligence," Travis told her, suddenly putting some of the pieces together. No wonder this man was skilled. No wonder Travis had had trouble ditching the tail and taking Ari in a fight. Mossad agents were highly trained, and he was glad this man was likely on their side. "Now I need to make a phone call to verify he's who he says he is."

She frowned at Ari. "And then do you need to make a phone call to verify he is who he says *he* is?"

Ari guffawed. "Your woman has a wonderful sense of humor."

Sandy looked from one man to the other and released a long-suffering sigh. "Men!" She said the word as if it had four letters, and that what she had to put up with was almost unbearable.

Travis shot a phone picture of Ari off to Kincaid. Within five seconds he had positive confirmation, since Mossad had just contacted Kincaid. Travis wasn't surprised any longer by his boss's contacts or how far and wide his rep was known. "His ID is corroborated."

Sandy immediately lowered the gun and handed it back to Ari. "Can you tell us anything about Ellie?"

Ari hesitated. "Not officially."

"Unofficially?" Travis asked.

"She's on Vanderpelt's island." Ari held up his hand to forestall more questions. "While we cooperate with the U.S., this investigation is...delicate."

"How delicate?" Travis asked.

"Let's put it this way—if my government didn't owe

Logan Kincaid a huge favor, this conversation wouldn't be taking place."

"Got it." Travis suspected Mossad had inserted a man onto the island. One wrong word, and the man's life could be compromised. That agent could very well be the man protecting Ellie, but he wouldn't blow his cover for her—not if other lives were at stake. "You have any idea why Vanderpelt wants these boats so badly?"

"After your people take apart the boat you left behind in the cove, we hope that your government might share whatever they find."

Travis shrugged. "That's not up to me. If Vanderpelt's hidden something on her, it's probably in the keel. Melting lead takes high temperatures. We could destroy whatever is hidden by trying to find it."

"Understood."

"Wait a second." Sandy frowned. "Aren't we turning over the boat we left in the cove to Dan and Randall tomorrow? Because if we don't, there's no telling what Vanderpelt might do to Ellie."

"First, he doesn't know that we took the place of the Canadian couple. Second, if this boat doesn't arrive, he'll need the next one even more. And third, tomorrow morning we are delivering the boat to Dan and Randall. Afterward, the U.S. Coast Guard is going to arrest them for drug smuggling."

"Huh?" Sandy looked confused, but Ari grinned.

"Drugs are now hidden in the bilge," Travis explained. "And so Vanderpelt cannot blame anyone but his own men for the screwup," Ari concluded. "The man is a master strategist."

Travis agreed. "If those guys know anything useful about Vanderpelt, they'll trade the information for lighter sentences. But I doubt they know much."

"What I don't understand is why Vanderpelt didn't use his own people to sail the boats to him," Sandy wondered aloud, clearly trying to figure out why she'd been drawn into this plot.

"Customs agents know you and your reputation," Ari explained. "Crossing the Canada/U.S. border is getting trickier. Both governments keep records that you deliver boats for a living and would have no reason to place you under close scrutiny. But a first-timer would be checked out. Not just the boat, but his background—and if he were caught, he might talk to the authorities. Why would Vanderpelt risk that when he could hire you?"

While Ari explained the likeliest scenario to Sandy, Travis's mind was working overtime. "I don't wish to put anyone in danger, but if your organization can contact my sister, please tell her that we're coming to take her home."

Ari gave Travis a long, hard, assessing look. His dark eyes seemed to pull into his skull. Then he dipped his head in a slight nod. Travis knew he would get no other acknowledgment that the message would be passed on to Ellie. That would have to be enough.

"Do you know Vanderpelt's real name?" Travis asked.

Ari shook his head. "He's a fanatic with connections that run deep into the pockets of the Saudi royals. He runs guns, heroin and white slaves. But he's always five steps removed from the action. This time, we fear he's setting up some kind of terrorist attack."

"On Israel, or the United States?" Sandy asked.

"We don't know." Ari's voice turned hard. "We need to find out to stop him."

"Why do you suspect him of international terrorism?" Travis asked, knowing that Ari would share what he could. Travis would bet a month's pay the Mossad knew much more than Ari was revealing.

"Because this time Vanderpelt's personally involved. Not even his closest associates know what is going on. But he's tightened security and distanced himself from even his longtime associates." Ari shook Travis's, then Sandy's, hand. "If you need to contact me, Kincaid knows how to reach me."

Travis wanted to ask the Mossad agent why he'd been following them, but Ari probably wouldn't answer that question.

ELLIE'S STOMACH GROWLED with hunger. She hadn't eaten in almost twenty-four hours. No one had visited her. It was as if Vanderpelt and his men had forgotten they were keeping her locked up.

When Alan unlocked the door, he entered her room with the Frenchman. One man held a rope, the other a blindfold. Her stomach cramped, this time not from hunger but fear.

"What is it?" she asked.

"Turn around," the Frenchman ordered.

"Why?"

"Just do it." Alan's eyes remained stony. Looking at him sent another dart of fear into her heart.

Ellie saw no chance to escape. She couldn't overpower two large men, both of them armed. Frustrated, trembling, she did as she'd been told.

Quickly, they trussed her hands behind her back, pulled the hood over her face and marched her out the door, each man gripping one of her arms. Mouth dry with fear, knees almost buckling, she wondered if they were going to kill her.

When Alan marched her up steps, she bit her lip to keep from begging. However, when he yanked off the hood, she found herself not on a scaffolding with a noose around her neck, or with a gun aimed at her head, but on a private deck that was surrounded by six-foot-high fencing.

A feast of roasted chicken, steamed vegetables, potatoes, assorted fruits and cheeses, plus several dishes of rich pasta sat on a picnic table. At the delicious aromas, her mouth watered. The two men departed without a word, leaving her hands tied behind her back.

She yanked on her wrists, unable to free them, wondering what was going on. Almost hungry enough to try eating with her hands tied, Ellie looked behind her, where Alan and the Frenchman had closed a sliding glass door. And she was facing the door when Vanderpelt arrived with a disappointed look in his eyes, as if he'd hoped to catch her in an embarrassing moment. Pride made her straighten her back, even as her stomach growled.

Vanderpelt took a seat in the only chair at the table, and floated a napkin onto his lap. "So good of you to join me."

Like she had a choice. Did he intend for her to stand there and watch him eat? The scents teased her nostrils, but the leer in Vanderpelt's eyes made her wary. Had he brought her here for no more reason than to toy with her? She watched him silently.

He broke off a piece of crusty bread, slathered it with butter and popped the morsel into his mouth. As he chewed slowly, she picked a spot above his right ear and stared at it. She might have no choice about breathing in the delicious aromas, and listening to him chew and swallow, but she didn't have to watch.

And she damn well wouldn't beg.

Chapter Ten

Vanderpelt had expected to find Ellie with her face buried in the food. Instead, she stood as still as a deactivated robot, her eyes glued somewhere over his head. At first, he thought she was losing it. But then he realized that she was defying him, and pleasure heated him.

At any other time, he would have enjoyed taming her slowly. Nothing pleased him more than breaking a woman's spirit. The sheer power thrilled him, and the ultimate yielding was one of the sweetest joys a man could experience.

But he didn't have time.

His mission was critical.

Between the damn U.S. Coast Guard that had confiscated his boat, and the storm threatening to blow his plans, he didn't have time for the finesse required to break a woman like Ellie. Still, he could enjoy the time he had.

Dabbing his mouth with a napkin, he eased back in his chair to stare at her. With her shoulders squared, her chin high and her spine so straight she could have been a soldier, she revealed the tension of battle. Oh, she might not be fighting with her fists, but she was resisting speaking, resisting the food, resisting *him.*

Vanderpelt didn't like for beautiful women to ignore him. Shoving back his chair, he stood and approached her. At his sudden action, her eyes flickered with wariness. A muscle in her jaw pulsed. Her lips tightened. She was magnificent in her resistance.

If he'd had more time, he would have let her stand and watch every meal he ate until she begged for food. Knowing it was too soon for her to yield to her own hunger, he simply gripped her arm and forced her to the table. Again, he took the only chair, but this time he toppled her.

Eyes wide, she let out a gasp as she fell.

And when he caught her in his lap, he saw her relief, then her anger. She'd totally skipped fear.

But that would soon change.

"Did you think I would let you fall?"

She stared at him. No, she stared through him, looking past his face as if it wasn't there.

"You will eat from my hand."

She didn't move. She didn't speak. Every muscle in her body was already tense, but somehow she stiffened even more. And then she relaxed, threw back her head and chuckled.

Once again, he considered whether the isolation had made her crazy. But Vanderpelt was a careful man, a man who studied people. And once again he saw the intelligence in her eyes that told him she was very much her own person.

Irritated that she gave him nothing, not even the respect of fear, he picked up a piece of chicken. "Open your mouth."

She chuckled at him, doing as he asked.

"I'm placing this on your tongue. If you chew before I give you permission, you will regret it."

She held perfectly still, waiting for his signal. Although she obeyed him, he sensed something was wrong. As if the little contest of wills meant nothing to him, he finally told her to chew. When she swallowed, he would slap her across the face for failing to wait for his next order.

However, the American witch seemed to read his mind. She chewed, and then she spit the chicken in his face.

Another man would have lost his temper. Vanderpelt was not such a man. Wiping the mess from his cheek, he stared at her for several long seconds. She didn't squirm, but she tugged at the tight bonds that tied her wrists. He smiled. "That was a mistake."

KINCAID HAD COME THROUGH on his promise to refit the sailboat. A thorough inspection had revealed the quality of the workmanship. From finely sanded and artfully stained mahogany cabinetry, to polished chrome stanchions, to the latest in navigational equipment, the boat appeared good as new. Still, Sandy held her breath after Travis raised a large jib and she turned off the wind, filling both the jib and mainsail. The boat heeled to starboard, putting pressure on the mast. If she didn't hold, it was better to find out here, while they were close to land, than during a storm, and miles from any safe harbor. The mast Kincaid's men had repaired from the stolen boat clanged and clanked and creaked as if in protest, but she held.

Sandy balanced the tiller with her knee as she winched in a sheet, tightening the sail and upping their speed half a knot. While Kincaid's crews recovered the boat in the cove and melted the sailboat's keel inch by inch, she and Travis would sail Vanderpelt's original, refitted vessel, beat the storm and reach Ellie. Since meeting the Mossad agent, Travis had been in a better mood, but neither he nor Sandy would be back to normal until they knew his sister was safe.

Back to normal.

Sandy didn't know what that meant, exactly. Would Travis return to his job, and she to hers, and pretend they'd never made love? Would their time together just be one more memory added to their old ones? With the breeze in her hair, sunshine on her face and the salty tang of sea in her lungs, she didn't know what she wanted. But just being out on the water eased the heaviness in her heart that had been there since Ellie's disappearance.

Sandy had been born in February, under the sign of

Aquarius. The water bearer. While she didn't know if she believed in astrology, she liked living by the water. She couldn't imagine living inland, where she couldn't sail on the endless stretch of the Atlantic Ocean. Her need for the freedom to come and go, sometimes for weeks at a time while she delivered a boat, might have interfered with her social life, preventing her from forming any permanent attachments to a man. Yet, she lived the life she loved.

"A penny for your thoughts." Travis leaned back in the cockpit and peered over his sunglasses at her.

"I could never give up the sea. It's in my blood."

"That's why you were smiling like a sexy vixen with a come-hither gleam in your eyes?"

"I was not." She sighed at his teasing. "Ease the jib a notch, please. Wind's going east."

Travis adjusted the line and secured it. "You feel any problems with the rudder?"

"She's good. And the mast's holding strong and straight. The stays are creaking a bit but the deck isn't flexing. Your boss hires—"

"Only the best." He tipped the brim of his cap and chuckled. "Glad you don't have any complaints."

Just like that, he'd turned the conversation personal. It wasn't so much his words as his intonation. If she hadn't known him for as long as she had, she might have missed his meaning.

She eyed him. One thing about Travis—around him she was never bored. He might be less ready to explode these days, but that didn't mean he wasn't unpredictable. Or charming. Or persistent. "I told you my thoughts, now you tell me yours."

His voice was low, sexy and playful. "I was thinking we should try the autopilot and then test the double bed."

She raised an eyebrow, but her heartbeat accelerated. "Beds don't require testing, do they?"

"Sure they do. First we need to see if the sheets fit. Then we need to see if we fit."

Travis could be as clever with words as he was with his hands. And the memory of his hands on her caused her breath to hitch. If another man threw double entendres at her the way Travis did, she might tell him off. She certainly wouldn't be this intrigued. But she wanted Travis. And that made all the difference. Old memories, and new ones, held him close to her heart. Knowing he also wanted her was like adding oil to embers, and the flaring heat drew her.

"The *only* place we fit is in bed," she countered, pleased her tone was much firmer than her wavering resolve.

"That was very true—the operative word being *was*."

She couldn't resist poking at his temper. "Have you forgotten how angry you were with me about Ari? Or, for that matter, when I didn't follow your instructions to hide in the dark when that ex-veteran pulled a shotgun on you?"

Travis's voice was mild, his tone intense. "Every couple fights."

"So now we're a couple?"

"We're that, and more. Even you can't deny that we care about one another."

"That's not enough. We aren't compatible."

"Because we argue?" Travis chuckled. He changed sides of the cockpit and sat beside her, drawing an arm over her shoulders. "Tell me you don't want to kiss me. Tell me you feel nothing for me, and I'll go fiddle with the engines. Tell me you wouldn't rather be together than alone right now, and you'd be a liar."

He knew her too well. She refused to look at him. "That's not the point. Don't you think we should focus solely on rescuing Ellie?"

"And use her as an excuse to ignore what's happening between us?"

"Nothing's happening," Sandy countered.

"You wouldn't have made love with me if you didn't have feelings for me." He held up a hand. "And I'm not talking about lust. Admit it, you worry about me. You think about me more often than you want to acknowledge."

"So? What does that give us? A whole lot of worrying, a nice memory to recall during old age—"

"Nice?" Insult colored his tone. "Making love to me was...*nice?*"

"What? Now, you need compliments? You were better than nice. You were great, okay. So what?" She challenged him to come up with words that would allow her to do what she wanted—which was to go below and make love to him.

"What more do you want from me?" Travis asked, keeping his tone conversational.

"That's just it Travis. You've already given everything you have to give—and it's not enough." If he didn't understand that caring and lovemaking were different from love and commitment, saying the words wouldn't clear the air. She'd only hurt him. And why throw ideals in his face when she hadn't the slightest idea what she wanted.

If Travis told her he loved her enough to stay, enough to marry her and try to have a life together, he'd be miserable. And so would she. Sandy wasn't the kind of woman who could do that to a man she cared for as deeply as she did Travis. Everything she loved about him would slowly die if he committed to her. It would be like caging a wild bird. She couldn't live with clipping his wings any more than she could give up the sea. There was no future for them. She knew it. He had to know it.

And yet, what harm would it do to take a few hours of pleasure in his arms? He wanted her. She wanted him. Vanderpelt might kill them when they arrived. Was she being foolish to hold back on some stupid ideal that wasn't even clear in her own mind?

Travis kissed her cheek. "You have underestimated me. I have more to give than you know."

"Then show me." The words came out before she could hold them back. But she didn't regret them. She would take these next few days, make the most of them and live with the consequences. She wouldn't draw back out of fear, or vulnerability, or scruples. Life was simply too short not to take this moment and live it.

SANDY ENGAGED THE self-steering gear and set their course, and Travis went below. When she joined him, she was surprised to see he'd dimmed the lamps and turned on the stereo, and had already switched the kitchen table back into a queen bed with sheets, pillows and blankets. "Wow. You sure know how to set a scene for seduction."

Travis, still dressed in jeans, but shirtless, drew her to him. His bronzed chest gleamed under the soft lighting, his powerful shoulders and arms an acute contrast to his sharp cheekbones. The cabin's ceiling cleared his head by two inches, so standing upright was comfortable. He opened his arms and gathered her against his chest. Usually, just his touch ignited a firestorm of need in her. But now, with the boat rocking beneath them and causing more friction than usual, she sensed an underlying tenderness in his gaze, in his unhurried movements, in the simmering heat of his expression.

"This time's going to be different," Travis promised, his tone a husky mix of hunger and self-control.

Tipping her head up, she wound her arms around his neck and threaded her fingers through his dark hair. "I don't have any complaints."

"Mmm." He kissed her brow, her nose, her lips. "We're always in a rush. I want to make this last."

His words, so full of promise, stoked her desire. But questions nagged. When they made love at their fast and furious pace, he left her no time to think, no time for doubts. And though she'd come to him sure she wanted to make love again, she didn't want to think anymore. She didn't want to second-guess her decision. She simply wanted to enjoy how good they were together.

"I'm...not...sure..." she began.

"I am." The certainty in his tone told her he had made up his mind, and a shimmy of anticipation raced down her spine. Earlier she'd reminded herself that being with Travis was always interesting. Well, right now, his cryptic comments held her fascinated and captive.

She began to remove her shirt. Already she ached to press her bare flesh against his chest. But he held her close, demanding, "Kiss me."

Unlike most women, who adored kissing, Sandy looked at making out as a warm-up to lovemaking—the good stuff. However, no one could kiss the way Travis did. As his breath merged with hers, as their lips tangled and their tongues tangoed, she could have sighed with the joy of him.

When Travis rushed her in eagerness, he was fantastic, but when he took his time...he was indescribably delicious. Little prickles of heat zipped along her neck. Her stomach knotted, and she found herself raising on her toes to have more of him.

And when his palms slid upward from her waist to her breasts, she wished desperately that she'd removed her shirt and bra. However, even with material between his fingers and her aching breasts, he caused her breath to rasp, and she arched into his hands.

She had no idea how long he kissed her while he played with her breasts. But he seemed willing to do so until she was ready to scream. The sensual, slow circles of his thumbs across her nipples had made her crave more of him. Out of breath, she pulled back. Her lips, already sensitive from his kisses, couldn't seem to form words.

She tugged at her T-shirt. "Let me take off—"

He placed his hands over hers. "Let me."

Sandy didn't care who removed what. She just wanted her clothes off before she melted down. He reached for her shirt and lifted it an inch to reveal a sliver of her tummy and back. Then, kneeling, he kissed and caressed her flesh until she trembled for more.

"Travis, we don't have all day."

"Yes. We do." He chuckled, a warm breath of air caressing her stomach.

"But. This is—"

"Heaven," he murmured, pulling her shirt over her head, leaving her standing in jeans and bra.

She thought he would remove her bra, but as usual, Travis was unpredictable. He nipped through the material at her nipples while his hands stroked her back, her shoulders and her collarbone.

Unable to stand another moment of such sweet torture, she unclasped her bra, tossed it onto the deck and attempted to unsnap her jeans. Travis frowned and turned away. "Do we have a spare line down here?"

"In the starboard locker. Why?"

"Because if you can't hold still…"

Her lower jaw dropped open in shock and titillation. "You wouldn't?"

"I will if you keep rushing me."

"I don't like threats." But her nipples tightened into buds so hard, she caught her breath, his idea making her throat hitch. To be totally at his mercy. The idea stretched her boundaries. Her sense of self. Her sense of trust.

"I want to give you pleasure," he told her, and she didn't doubt him. But still…

"You always give me pleasure," she countered. "And I'm not ready to play that kind of game."

"But you're interested."

It wasn't a question. He'd made the statement with a knowing gaze, and a confidence that left her floundering. How could he read her so well? And then she caught sight of herself in a mirror. Her eyes were wide and wild. Her lips bee-stung, and her nipples taut.

"Travis, don't push me on this," she told him.

"Okay." He came closer, close enough for her to feel the heat radiating off his skin. Close enough to see the flecks of dark green in the circles around his irises. Close enough to smell his masculine scent. "But will you at least try and hold still for me?"

Frustration and exasperation filled her. She was ready now. "What's the point?"

His hands cupped her breasts gently. "Let me show you."

And he did.

And she'd never felt so cherished. Never. Every caress brought her pleasure. And each stroke, every tender nuzzle, heightened her lust. Only this wasn't just lust. He was loving her with his hands and his lips. And his heart?

The idea scared her. Exhilarated her. And she tucked

it away to think about later, when she had more of her wits about her.

Right now, she just wanted him to take off the rest of her clothes. He'd asked her to let *him* do that. And she would honor that request. But he'd said nothing about her not taking off his jeans.

Usually, they flung their clothes off with no finesse. Sometimes buttons popped. But as she reached for his waistband, teasing his skin with her fingertips and hearing his hiss of air, she realized there was something to this slowing down. The longer burning time allowed the skin to grow more flushed, the heart to pound faster, the cravings to sharpen.

Ever so slowly, she unfastened the buttons of his jeans, her task made ever more difficult by his arousal that pulled the fabric tight. Her own blood licked through her veins like heated wine. Her trembling fingers seemed to take forever to break the condom packet and unroll it over him, but she enjoyed caressing him, teasing him as she did so, fondling his shaft and taking satisfaction in his soft groans.

Finally when they both stood before one another naked, he guided her to the bunk. She expected him to pick up the pace. But he seemed just as determined to make sure that not one inch of her flesh went untended by his fingertips and his lips.

When her breath came in huge gulps, when her heart raced, when the need for him grew unbearably strong, she told herself she could wait just one more minute, one more moment. Longing for just a caress between her thighs, she parted her legs. Travis, however, might have a fierce urgency in his taut body, but he also had a savage control.

His mind was set. So she'd just have to change it.

"Travis."

"Mmm."

"Travis." She gripped his hair and tugged his mouth from her breasts. "I've waited long enough."

"Okay."

She thought he would grab her hips and sheathe himself inside her. But he didn't. He dipped his head back to her breasts and swirled his tongue over her until she was flush with heat, taut with tension.

She tried to twist away, to get a moment's relief from the mounting pressure. "Travis. I mean…it."

"I know."

She wanted to scream in frustration. Pound his back. Dig her nails into his skin. Holding still, letting him set this ridiculously slow pace, was driving her mad.

"I want you now."

"Soon," he promised with a soft chuckle.

"Now."

"Such impatience."

"Travis—"

"Yes." With one hand, he grabbed her wrists and held them over her head.

She squirmed under him, arching, spreading her thighs, desperate to take him inside her.

"Do you trust me?" he demanded.

"Now's…one helluva time…to…" Finally, he

reached between her legs, parting her folds, his touch so light, so gentle. "Ah…Ah…"

"Do you trust me?"

She raised her head, stared into his glittering eyes. "Yes. Damn you."

"Then hold still for me."

"I can't."

"For just a little bit longer?"

His eyes promised the wait would be worth it. Biting her bottom lip, she nodded, summoning willpower from she knew not where. "Okay."

Releasing her hands, he moved down her body. And then his tongue found her sensitive core. Despite her promise, holding still was impossible. She thrashed, reached for him. His hands came up and his fingers interlocked with hers.

And as the boat rose and fell with the waves, she came so close to completion that she let out small whimpers from the back of her throat with the wonder of him.

"Travis…please."

"Soon." He either whispered the words again or she heard them in her mind. And the exquisite sensations were overriding thought, overriding good sense, shooting her over the edge of control.

He kept her poised on the brink for so long that when he finally filled her with one smooth thrust, the wave broke over her, one crest after another. But he didn't stop moving, and neither did her orgasm that invoked every cell in her body and blew her mind wide open. Never had she known such pleasure was possible. And as she clung to Travis, riding the last wondrous contractions, she wondered how she'd ever let him go.

Chapter Eleven

Sandy would have liked to spend the entire day with Travis, making love and getting to know this giving side of him. He'd been right about one thing—slowing down had brought them both an enormous amount of pleasure. The waiting, the anticipation, had allowed not just her physical arousal to build, but the emotional awakening, as well.

It wasn't as if she hadn't always had feelings for Travis. And she knew he had them for her, too. But before, their feelings were like a swift-running stream. This had been plumbing the depths of a deep tidal pool, and she savored the closeness.

However, the winds had picked up. The rocking boat keeled over on its leeward side. Weather called them topside. While Travis used the communications system and checked in with Kincaid, Sandy noted thick, billowing clouds of dark gray that blocked not only the sun, but the sky from one horizon to the other.

The rushing winds increased their speed, but if the storm kept approaching at this rate, within hours the waves would begin to slow them down. Travis handed her a foul-weather jacket, his face grim. "Our current course will place us on the outer perimeter of the hurricane. Gusts estimated at seventy-five to ninety-five miles an hour. Seas ten to fifteen feet."

Donning the jacket, she tried to keep the worry from her face. "What are our choices?"

"Head straight to the island and hope we make the harbor before the storm. Or we could turn back. Or change our heading and hold up somewhere at sea until the storm passes."

"I think we should nix the last option." Sandy pulled in the tiller and adjusted their heading. "We should either return to the mainland or keep going, because if we try to wait out the storm at sea, it could change direction and find us anyway."

Travis nodded. "Kincaid says it's our call. The U.S. Coast Guard's advanced Search and Rescue has been notified of our situation, and that we may require assistance."

The thought didn't comfort Sandy. She knew all too well that rescue helicopters couldn't fly in hurricane winds. If they capsized, they wouldn't be rescued until after the storm passed. Under that scenario, the capsized boat would leave them, at best, in the dinghy, at worst, floating in life vests. And even if they survived, even if the Coast Guard knew their position when they went down, they might never be found. And where would that leave Ellie?

The hurricane left their options bleak. "Either way, we need to change the jib, soon. And reef the main. I don't want to get caught with too much sail up and risk the mast."

Travis sat next to her. "We need to decide this together."

Sandy's gut tightened into a line of knots. Only a fool wouldn't fear to sail down the throat of a hurricane's path—especially with a boat that had suffered the kind of damage this one had. "Is there enough time to head back, wait out the storm and still make Vanderpelt's deadline after the hurricane passes?"

"Maybe. Depends how long the system takes to go by. Hurricanes are unpredictable."

"What do you think?" Sandy asked him, wanting his opinion. As much as she trusted her seamanship, Travis had other concerns on his mind and would see a bigger picture. No doubt, he understood better what help Kincaid could give them, and the capabilities of the Coast Guard.

"If we can arrive right before the storm, we might take Vanderpelt by surprise. He certainly won't be expecting us so soon. And, in our favor, the high seas, rain and low clouds may hide our approach. The storm might be the edge we need to get Ellie away safely."

She understood Travis was trying to turn the situation to his advantage. But was his decision one of loving brother who couldn't bear to lose his sister, or one of a man who believed they had a real chance to succeed? She searched his eyes for the answer. "You want to go, don't you?"

He shrugged. "We're putting our lives on the line. If you want to turn back, it still might be the best option."

But he didn't think so. Of course, he was guessing. With the storm so unpredictable, it could stall, change direction or forge ahead. Whatever they decided would be a gamble. But if Travis thought Ellie's best chance was for them to keep going, Sandy didn't want to ask him to turn back. Although they would most certainly live if they came about and headed for land, she didn't know if she could go on after such a decision—especially if Ellie didn't make it because they'd missed Vanderpelt's deadline.

She leaned forward to kiss Travis, her mind made up. "Let's go get Ellie, now."

He pulled back, looking deep into her eyes, clearly concerned for her. "You're sure?"

"Yeah." But in truth, she was only sure about one thing—her heart was too full to disappoint him. If that was bad decision-making, so be it. "Now kiss me, quick."

He kissed her. But it wasn't quick. The new tenderness he'd revealed while they'd made love told her she hadn't been mistaken about Travis. Their earlier passion hadn't blinded her to a deepening of their attachment to one another.

Drawing back, she opened a locker and dumped the safety gear into his lap. "From now on, if we're on deck, we need to be tied in with an overboard line. And—" she handed him a life vest "—wear this, too."

He winked at her. "Aye, aye, Captain."

Heartache lifting at the choice they'd just made, she turned into the wind, luffing the sails. As he pulled down the jib and replaced it with a tiny storm sail, she kept the bow pointed into the wind and was glad the decision was over. She much preferred action to angst. Then, together they reefed the mainsail. Despite the reduction in canvas, with the steadily increasing winds, they sped over the waves, their wake frothing behind them with churning bubbles. But the crests kept rising, the troughs deepening, the water's color darkening to inky blue, and now the waves were almost as high as the mast. They'd surf down a wave, and she had to turn the bow at an angle to avoid burying it in the next one.

She'd sailed in weather like this only once before and was pleased with the way the boat handled. Kincaid's team had really done a super job of putting her back together.

While Sandy remained at the tiller, Travis went below. He returned about twenty minutes later with hot coffee, thick turkey sandwiches and cookies. She hadn't realized how hungry she was until after she began to eat and finished every bite. After hours of lovemaking, and now facing this storm, their bodies needed refueling and there was no telling when they would eat again.

"Any news?"

He shook his head. "Kincaid has the boat we left in the cove on a cradle and they are trucking her to a factory that's equipped to deal with melting the lead. The storm is in a holding pattern. And nothing significant turned up on Dan and Randall. They're just second-tier freelance employees who have no idea what's really going on."

Sandy Travis were sailing almost due east, hoping to reach the island before they intersected with the storm coming up from the south. While the huge weather system was moving slowly, they were sailing closer, hence the larger waves and the windy conditions. Although she enjoyed her stint at the helm, her arms ached from the pull of the tiller, and she had no doubt that the strain between her shoulder blades would worsen before the day ended.

"Want to relieve me for a while?" she asked, knowing she needed to save her strength in case the storm's fury caught up with them.

"Sure."

Travis took the tiller and she stretched to ease the kinks from her shoulders, neck and thighs. With her muscles somewhat relaxed, she stowed winches in the cockpit, making sure that if they heeled hard or took a wave over the bow that they wouldn't lose critical equipment. Meanwhile, she watched Travis closely. He was a weekend sailor—a good one, but he hadn't her experience. She doubted he'd sailed in these kinds of gale-like conditions, yet he held a steady course while evading the critical mistake of burying the bow into the next oncoming wave.

Relieved that he had the boat under control, she went

below, checked her navigational instruments, then continued to stow loose objects. Nothing was worse than coming below in a storm for an hour's rest and being clobbered by a tool, a glass or a book. While furniture and most equipment had already been secured by the boat's designers, there were always other things like pens, charts and clothing that needed putting away. With the boat rocking and heeling over, she took longer than she would have liked to neaten the cabin. Not only was she worried about losing a critical item, but also that any object that came loose could smash a porthole. And once water started coming in, valuable equipment like computers and radios would suffer irreparable damage.

In addition, she placed Travis's cell phone in a dry box, which she tucked in an emergency duffel bag that hung by the hatch. Inside the bag were food, water, flares, fishing equipment, a medical kit and a GPS device that signaled satellites of their location. In an emergency, if they had to abandon ship for the life raft, the contents of that bag could keep them alive until rescuers found them—if they didn't drown first.

"Sandy!"

Travis had raised his voice to be heard over the roaring wind, the creaking boat and the rushing waves. However, she detected trouble in his tone.

"I'm coming." Navigating the four steps from the cabin deck back to the cockpit wasn't usually a problem, however, as a precautionary measure, she'd closed in the bottom of the hatch with boards. If they took water into the open cockpit, she wanted as little as possible to enter the cabin below. So climbing out, with the seas rolling, was more difficult than usual.

The boat designers had anticipated her problem, and sturdy handrails helped her efforts. Still, she had to time her movements to when the boat leveled on a crest. Travis steadied her the last few steps and then she tied herself in with safety gear. The moment she came topside, wind whipped at her hair and salt spray lashed her face. Inside her foul-weather gear she remained warm and dry, except for her hands and face that the sea splashed with regularity.

"We're going too fast." Travis told her. "I'm almost overpowered. If the wind—"

He'd called her too late. She could feel the vibration of the deck under her thighs, sense the stress on the hull. The tiny storm jib blew out, the sail flapping in tatters.

Automatically, she reached for the tiller. "There's a sea anchor in the locker. We need to slow down."

He moved to do as she asked, but yelled back over his shoulder, "You don't want to take down any more sail?"

"If we do, I'll lose rudder control." However, if they didn't slow the boat down, the stress on the hull would be enormous. The best way to survive these kinds of waves was to simply float like a cork. But the boat was too big for that. A cork only dealt with one wave at a time. The boat was large enough to be caught between the waves and the wind. No matter how strong Kincaid's people had rebuilt her, man-made objects weren't made to withstand the forces of nature.

Travis struggled with the locker, fought with the sea

anchor, too. Between the pitching boat, the wind and the constant sea shower, every movement took extraordinary effort and care. His progress slowed further as the skies opened up and icy rain drenched them, making the decks more slippery. Sandy tried to ignore the lightning bolting from boiling dark thunderclouds in the distance. At least with the seas so high, the mast wasn't towering above the ocean. Still, metal attracted lightning....

Travis deployed the sea anchor. The tiny parachute device filled with water and immediately slowed them. It also steadied the boat, enough that she knew one of them could go on deck to take down the torn jib. Still, she debated leaving it up and cutting it down later. But the flapping line of the tangled and tattered front sail was slapping the mainsail, interfering with the stays that connected the mast to the deck.

"I'll go." Travis snapped his safety line to a cleat and, hand over hand, made his way onto the slippery deck. She held her breath, held the boat steady and prayed he wouldn't lose his grip. If he fell overboard, she couldn't turn back, couldn't slow down without capsizing the boat.

If he went over the side, the only way she'd have to haul him in was by the line attached to his harness. She didn't have the strength to reel him in like a fish, but she could use the mechanical advantage of the winch. However, balancing the tiller and winching him in would be next to impossible.

She held her breath, keeping one eye on the water, one on him. Travis didn't attempt to stay on his feet. His progress was spiderlike, using hands and feet at different angles. He loosened the line at the mast to release the sail to the deck. A wave washed over the bow, tangling the mess even further.

"Cut it loose," she screamed. She didn't know if he heard her, but when he finally traversed onto the deck, he pulled out the knife strapped to his ankle. Holding on to a stanchion with one hand, he sawed at the thick, salty-wet line with his knife. That's when a giant wave washed over the bow, lifting him off the deck.

Oh, God, no.

Sandy could do nothing but scream and hold the tiller steady. As the bow cut through the wave, she blinked away the rain and salt spray. Despite his bright yellow foul-weather gear, she didn't see Travis.

He was gone.

Washed overboard between beats of her heart.

She didn't bother searching the water for him. Instead, she followed the direction of his lifeline. But it was still leading forward toward the bow.

Had she run him over after the wave washed him into the sea? Was he drowning, caught on his line somewhere under the boat? If she tried winching him in, she might do more damage than good.

Her heart raced and her hands went icy. Forcing huge gulps of air into her lungs, she stayed at the helm, trying not to panic, taking the next wave and praying that Travis could somehow climb up that rope.

That's when she spotted his hand clinging to the rail. And the next wave lifted him and floated him back onto the deck, where he clung precariously, like a cowboy on a bucking and twisting bull. Every atom in her body screamed to leave the helm and go to him. But self-navigation gear was meant for calmer waters and couldn't cope with these waves. If she left her position, the boat would turn broadside and roll.

She understood that for him to stay afloat as his foul-weather gear filled with water, and pull himself back onto the deck had taken superhuman strength. He had to be resting.

But was he injured? The waves could have slammed him into the boat. She watched him clinging to the deck, and she had no idea if all his ribs were broken, or if he'd suffered internal injuries.

And the gray sky was turning ugly purple-black. The wind stung her eyes along with the sea, and her tears couldn't keep the sting out. Her hand on the tiller was so cold, she could no longer feel her fingers. But right now, all her concern was for Travis.

"Move," she shouted, but the wind swallowed her words before she could hear them, and the sound couldn't possibly have reached Travis.

Yet, he moved. He drew his knees under him and, inch by inch, he crawled from the bow to the stern. She had no idea how long it took him to reach her, but as he tumbled into her arms, she held him close. She'd thought she'd lost him and the sick feeling in her gut had barely started to ease before his lips found hers.

She needed his kiss to tell her that he was okay, that together they would survive—the storm, the island and whatever Vanderpelt threw their way. Believing in him helped her regain her optimistic attitude. Surely, they'd come through the worst. But as he kissed her hard, the thunder overhead echoed ever closer.

"Are you hurt?" she shouted, even though he was mere inches from her.

He signaled her a thumbs-up and shot her one of his daring grins. More than any words, that grin reassured her and much of the tension inside her heart eased.

"I'm changing course," she told him, heading away from the storm and veering north of Vanderpelt's island. The boat couldn't take this kind of lashing, and more importantly, neither could they. One loose handhold, and the pitching boat could slam them into the hull, breaking bones. Or worse.

Travis didn't argue and the course change made the ride immediately smoother. They could have a conversation now, although they still had to speak more loudly than normal.

"We're making fantastic time," she told him. "Why don't you go below and change out of those wet clothes?"

"I'm fine."

"Travis, you won't do Ellie any good if you're sick when we arrive. Go change."

"Aye, aye, Captain."

He rejoined her after a few minutes and shoved a cup of hot chocolate into her hands. She let the heat burn down her throat and gave him the once-over. He was moving stiffly, but his eyes remained calm. She hoped he'd taken some aspirin. "Did you get Kincaid on the phone?"

"The storm is playing havoc with traffic along the coast. Hundreds of thousands of people are evacuating. The boat we left in the cove was hauled by the Coast Guard to a harbor and lifted onto a truck, and is now stuck in traffic due to people fleeing. However, Kincaid obtained a map of the island from the carpenter who worked for Vanderpelt. He says there's a house, a couple of outbuildings nearby. It's his guess Vanderpelt's men bunk in one of them and that Ellie might be in another. There's an airstrip on the far side of the island with several more buildings."

"Did he know how many men Vanderpelt employs?"

"He's guessing anywhere from three to twenty-five." Travis leaned back to shield her from salt spray. "Overhead satellite shots revealed at least five men. The clouds are blocking the island now, so we're going in blind."

"Hey, if we can't see them, they can't see us. And they aren't expecting us early. Right?" She sensed that the closer they drew to Ellie, the more difficult it was for him to tamp down his worries.

Although the boat was riding the waves better in this direction, the calm was deceptive. The storm had gained on them, and it was difficult for her to remember it was only late afternoon when the sky resembled a gloomy dusk.

From above and behind them, a bolt of lightning flashed like a spear, the high mast its target. Lightning struck nearby. From out of the depths of the ocean, a huge rushing roar drew Sandy's horrified gaze.

A wave of gigantic size crested before them, the towering wall of water menacing from a height at least three times higher than the sailboat's mast. Travis locked his arms around her and then all hell broke loose. The bow rode up, and up, like a ride at an amusement park.

"Oh, God!" she screamed, knowing there was no time to abandon ship, grab her emergency supplies and jump into the dinghy. The wave already had them in its clutches. "We're going over."

The wave pitchpoled the boat, tossing the bow over the stern.

The last thing Sandy heard before the sea enclosed her in its icy tentacles was the mast snapping like a twig and shrieking as if suffering a mortal wound. Before the spars and stays and metal toppled, she was underwater, Travis holding her close, his body pressing against hers. If the boat didn't do a three-sixty, neither of them would survive.

ELLIE PACED IN HER CELL, her nerves racing. Vanderpelt's expression after she'd spat the chicken in his face had been priceless. But then his surprise had turned to pleasure, and she realized he was getting aroused at her defiance.

He'd reached for her breast. She'd slammed her head into his face. Although she doubted she'd broken his nose, blood spurted. With an angry roar of pain, he'd dropped her onto the patio deck.

He had pulled back his foot to kick her, and she'd rolled. With her hands behind her back, regaining her feet was awkward, but she'd managed. Vanderpelt had stopped his abuse to grab a napkin from the table to soak up the blood.

And that's how Alan had found them.

She'd been in a crouch, ready to shift, retreat or advance, depending on Vanderpelt's next move. Her tormentor was scowling at her, blood dripping over his lips.

The sick bastard licked the blood, his eyes brightening as if he enjoyed it.

Alan entered the patio, took one look at her, then ignored her. "Sir, you should get ice on that right away, or you'll wake up with two black eyes."

She wished she'd done more damage. She would have liked to kick him in the groin, would have taken great pleasure in them ballooning to the size of grapefruits.

Alan had grabbed her arm and she'd let him. The Frenchman had joined them, and no way could she fight three men with her hands tied. Alan then shook her and shoved her through the patio doors. "I'll take care of this one," he'd said.

"No. Don't hurt her," Vanderpelt ordered. "I want that pleasure for myself."

Alan had taken her back to her cell. She'd been offered no food. And she had no idea when Vanderpelt would order his men to bring her to him again. She only knew that her stomach curled with dread.

Chapter Twelve

Travis's lungs burned like fire. He'd heard drowning wasn't a bad way to die, but the experts were wrong. He didn't feel at peace. He wasn't ready to let go. Ellie needed him. Sandy needed him. And as the enormous wave pummeled him, making it impossible to discern up from down, he clung to Sandy, determined not to lose her. When the water stopped churning, he struggled for the surface. If not for the bubbles rising from his mouth, he might not have known which direction to swim. Fighting against the frothing sea, the weight of his clothes and the cold, he swam toward the surface, exhausting his air supply. If Sandy hadn't been kicking madly beside him, he might not have found the strength to swim them up.

Usually, light from the surface beckoned. But in this case, the darkness around them seemed to have no end. When the pressure on his ears let up a little, encouraging him to keep going, he gritted his teeth to prevent himself from gulping water. Finally, his head popped through the surface, and Sandy and he breathed in giant swallows of air.

"You okay?" He coughed up some salt water and peered at her. Her skin was too pale, her eyes red-rimmed from the salt, her lips blue—and she'd never looked more beautiful. She was alive.

"Yeah, I'm okay. You take me to the most romantic places."

He looked for injuries but saw no bruises or blood on her head or neck. "You sound fine."

She spit salt water. "I'm great. I love swimming in the middle of the Atlantic Ocean during a hurricane. Wouldn't miss it for the world."

Another woman would have been hysterical. Sandy pulled on an inner strength that allowed her courage to come through in sarcasm. He shook his head and grinned.

They bobbed in the rough seas and he twisted, looking for the sailboat. The safety harnesses and lines tying them to the boat could have been severed, which might or might not have been a blessing if the boat had sunk without pulling them down with it.

They couldn't survive in the cold water more than a few hours before hypothermia would set in. Reaching for the safety line, he tugged, expecting to be able to reel it in with ease. But the line pulled taut.

And then the boat burst out of the water, keel side down, cabin side up.

"Look!" He tugged on Sandy's hand, praying for the strength to swim to the boat and climb aboard, but renewed by adrenaline and hope. "Let's go."

Hand over hand, they pulled themselves along the safety lines through the water, toward the boat. With her mast broken and her rigging hanging, the boat appeared battered, but she rode high in the water as if she'd taken on little of the sea. They had to take care not to tangle with the broken shrouds and stays, loose lines and assorted pieces of broken rigging.

Climbing into the boat would have been impossible if not for the safety line that Travis looped around a winch. Then, using his arms to pull himself up on the rope and bracing his feet against the hull, he hauled himself into the rocking boat. If he'd been in a swimsuit, the task would have been easier. With his clothes full of water, it took maximum effort. But even as he pulled himself over the side, he couldn't relax.

He found one winch handle miraculously still lodged in a cubby and used the mechanical advantage to pull Sandy aboard. Every muscle in him ached. His hands were raw, and both of them needed to raise their body temperatures. He had no idea how long they'd been drenched, but the toll made his movements sluggish, his brain sleepy.

"The bilge pump." Sandy flopped beside him and she seemed to be thinking more clearly than he. If they'd taken on water, and they must have, the water would flow to the lowest point—the bilge. Starting the pump to bail her was a necessity to staying afloat.

"I'll go see what I can do." From somewhere, he found the strength to shove to a sitting position. The sky had lightened. The water seemed calmer. He should have been reassured. But he wondered if they might be floating in the hurricane's eye. If so, they might have only a few minutes to make repairs before the winds and waves increased once more.

The cabin was surprisingly dry. She hadn't seemed to take in much seawater except where the mast had ripped a hole in the deck. Removing the floorboard, he checked the bilge for water. The damage from the broken mast had split parts of the deck, revealing a false floor.

Travis stared, rubbed his eyes and stared again. Despite his cold shivering, he began to sweat. Dropping to his knees, he carefully pried back the rest of the damaged area. "Sandy!" he yelled.

"Yeah?"

"There's a bomb on board."

"What!" She stuck her head inside the cabin and stared at him. "Did you say there's a bomb?"

"Yeah. Now we know why Vanderpelt wanted *this* boat. Vanderpelt must have paid off a carpenter to build a false deck under the bilge. If I'm not mistaken, we're delivering a bomb to Vanderpelt."

"We can't…" Sandy's hand rose up to her mouth as the ramifications slammed her. "But if we don't… Ellie…" She climbed down to stand next to him, misery in her eyes. "Travis, what are we going to do?"

"Find the satellite phone. I have to call Kincaid."

"But what if he orders you to come home?" Sandy asked but searched for the phone—not easy to do in the mess. Although they'd made the vessel shipshape, when the boat pinwheeled, cabinets had flown open, their contents strewn and tossed everywhere.

But his mind was on the bomb. Travis had had some extraordinary training during his time in the Special Forces. Kneeling, he looked at the wires, timing device and radioactive casing, but didn't touch. "The bomb components are U.S. military issue."

"You're sure?" Sandy asked, tossing aside plastic containers from her bunk in her search for the phone.

"Yeah. And I suspect what we have here is a dirty bomb."

She removed a box of garbage bags, a roll of aluminum foil and three spoons from the sink. "The kind that explodes and emits radiation? Isn't it illegal for the U.S. to have them?"

"The parts were stolen from the U.S. military. I suspect the americium was added later."

"Americium?"

"It's like plutonium, only easier to obtain."

"How much easier?"

"It's used on construction sites for soil testing. Twenty-two machines with americium were stolen from Florida in the last five years. Fifty-six from Texas—more than enough to make a dirty bomb."

"Or two dirty bombs?" Clearly, she was thinking about the other boat. "If they heat the bomb, will it explode?"

"No. They don't work that way." He didn't tell her the bombs could be set on a timer, triggered by remote control. "But I need to talk to Kincaid."

SANDY WENT FROM ICY cold to hot and back to icy cold. Where was the phone? Could the dry bag have floated through the deck hole next to the mast?

She checked under drawers that had fallen loose and cushions from the bunks that now blocked light from the portals, not even bothering to straighten as she searched. And all the while her fears for Ellie escalated. No way would any responsible person permit Travis to turn over a dirty bomb to a terrorist. Kincaid struck her as a man who would, by necessity, put the safety of hundreds of thousands of innocents against Ellie's and make a hard decision.

She couldn't imagine what Travis must be feeling right now. Desperation. Despair. Yet his expression held neither of those dark emotions. His eyes glowed with a fierce determination that told her he was far from giving up on saving Ellie.

She lifted a bumper that had fallen from a locker and spied the satellite phone's dry box. "Got it!"

Travis unsnapped the protective plastic, that would keep a phone dry even if fully submerged, and extracted the phone. She held her breath as he made the call and explained the situation in unemotional, efficient sentences.

He glanced at her and snapped the speaker option on so she could hear both sides of the conversation. "I'm no demolitions expert."

"You've a steady hand and can follow directions, can't you?"

Oh, no. Kincaid wanted Travis to dismantle the bomb?

"Travis?"

Travis was asking about the Shey pilot. Travis had once bragged to her how Jack had set them down during a blizzard in the middle of the Rocky Mountains.

"Not even Jack can fly in this kind of storm," Kincaid declared. "I'm connecting you to Jim, an expert in diffusing military bombs."

Sandy didn't want to hear more bad news. She started to leave the cabin before Travis saw her face pale or her hands tremble. Besides, she needed to figure out what to do with the rigging before they passed through the hurricane's eye.

"Sandy." Travis's voice stopped her. "Two pairs of eyes will be better than one."

"But..." He didn't need an argument from her right now. And if the bomb blew, it made no difference if she was beside him or topside. Because if it exploded, there wouldn't be enough of them left for fish food. Taking a deep, steadying breath, she nodded. "Okay."

"Put on some dry clothes, then hand me the toolbox," Travis suggested, and she prayed that he blamed her shivering on the cold rather than her nerves. Stepping carefully around the revealed bomb to the forward cabin, Sandy stripped, rubbed her skin briskly with a towel, then donned dry clothes. She shoved her wet hair into a wool cap and returned to hear a man asking Travis detailed questions.

"Black and red wires come out of the top," Travis said. "Yellow and green are at the bottom."

"You want to disconnect the blue one," Jim said.

Travis squatted on his heels, his voice deadly calm. "There is no blue one."

Her heart raced and sweat beaded on her forehead. Wishing she had something to do besides worry, she recalled Travis's request. Sandy found the toolbox in its regular locker below the stairs.

"Follow the yellow wire to its source."

"I'll have to remove more of the hull to see it."

Sandy meant to keep quiet but spoke up. "If you remove more of the fiberglass hull, the mast will lose support. Attaching a sail may become impossible, and with the storm returning, if we can't stabilize..."

"But if I can extract the bomb's core, we can deliver this boat to Vanderpelt."

"What will you do with the americium?" she asked.

"Put it in the lifeboat with a GPS beacon. The navy already has a ship on the way."

So he was giving away their life raft and weakening the hull, too. But it was the only chance they had to keep the bomb out of Vanderpelt's hands and to retrieve Ellie. If she'd thought their chance of success was slim when they'd started this mission, she now realized it was even less. However, she nodded her agreement and handed Travis a chisel from the toolbox so he could chip away at the hull.

"I'm trying to clear out some space under the wires, Jim," Travis told the bomb expert.

"Whatever you do, try not to jar the wires loose."

She didn't want to know why, but Travis did.

"Why not?"

"A loosened wire will automatically set the timer's clock ticking."

"Just in case...do we have a procedure to stop the timer?"

"Not without access codes or equipment you don't have."

"I'll be careful," Travis promised.

Sandy clasped one hand in the other, wishing she had something to do. Travis was lying on his stomach, his arms extended below the deck.

"Would a flashlight help?" she asked.

"Yeah."

She grabbed the light kept mounted to the wall for constant recharging. But her angles around Travis were limited, and no matter how she shined the light, she couldn't aim it so he could see.

"Is there a way to do this by touch?" Travis asked.

The other man hesitated, as if reluctant to give an answer. "The wire you want to cut should be a millimeter thicker than the one you mustn't cut."

A millimeter? Travis had yet to change clothes. His fingers had to be numb with cold and his hands were bleeding in a dozen places because they were too large for the opening.

"This isn't working, Jim." She spoke up. "He can't see his hands and the opening is too small for him to work."

"She's right." Travis stood up, unrolled a blanket

where he'd just been lying and gestured for her to take his place. "Your hands are smaller."

Was that a moan that came, unbidden, from her mouth? Or the wind keening outside?

Travis placed wire cutters in her hand. "Slip your fingers under the box, find the smaller wire and cut it."

She closed her eyes for a brief second to collect her wits. She'd thought having something to do would release the tension that almost froze her in place. But she'd been wrong. Now she had both their lives, and probably Ellie's, in her hands.

But she wasn't a quitter. Lying on her stomach, she eased her hands down and twisted them around the smooth metal that looked as innocuous as a suitcase.

"Take your time. Be careful not to jar the wires," Travis reminded her, his tone calm and steady, just like when he'd taught her to drive a stick shift.

"Can you feel the place where the wires come out of the box?"

"Yes. There are three of them."

"You're sure?" Jim asked, and from his tone she knew something was wrong.

"Yes."

"Can you see them?"

"No. My arm's stuck to the elbow under the box."

"Don't do anything. Don't move. I'm pulling up specs."

"Hey, don't worry, I won't even breathe."

Jim chuckled. Travis whistled as if he hadn't a care in the world. He tossed off his wet clothes and donned dry ones from a waterproof locker, and placed his foul-weather gear back on.

"Where do you think you're going?"

"To fix the rigging."

"Travis, if I cut the wrong wire—"

"You won't."

"We'll die. I'd like to be together if that happens."

"You're too stubborn and ornery to die. Besides, after you make the right choice, you have to sail us out of here. And to do that, you need a sail. I thought I'd try and brace the mast with pieces from the crossbracing."

Everything he said made sense, but she didn't want to cut that wire by herself. "Don't go."

"If you two are done arguing," Jim interrupted them, "I've found the specs. They stole something so classified, I hadn't seen it yet."

She groaned.

"Don't worry. This is going to be easier than you think. All you have to do is cut the middle wire."

"You're sure?" Travis asked.

"Yes."

"Okay. I have the middle wire between the wire cutters."

"Do it."

She closed her eyes and cut the wire. When nothing happened, she realized they were still alive. With a whoop of joy, Travis helped her up and kissed her. "Nice job."

In the background she could hear Jim chuckling, but all she could think about was the warmth in Travis's eyes that told her he was proud of her. And she no longer cared if Travis knew she was shaking. They could have died several times today. She had a right to her fears, as well as a right to take comfort and joy from a man she loved.

Loved?

The thought startled her. When the hell had that happened? She'd been determined not to repeat the mistakes of her past, to protect her heart, to make love without falling hard. And she'd failed miserably.

She supposed that as much as she thought of herself as a free spirit, she had old-fashioned values. She couldn't make love without her feelings being involved, and she couldn't spend this kind of intense time with a man without an emotional reaction.

Actually, the fighting and arguing had been at a minimum. Considering they'd faced death more than once, and that the pressure on both of them to save Ellie always simmered between them, they had gotten along quite well. There had been no screaming matches. No slamming doors. No ugly words of blame.

They'd worked together like a team. Who would have thought it?

Yet once they found Ellie, the bond that kept them together for a common purpose would dissolve. She'd have to deal with heartbreak over one man for a second time, and she wondered why the fates had brought them together again—except to mock them.

Travis must have sensed something of her feelings. He whispered, his husky voice reverberating in her ear. "What?"

She didn't want to speak about her newfound love for him. Now was not the time. It might never be the time. Although they were no longer fighting their way through every conversation, although they had both matured and no longer blamed one another for every little thing that went wrong, that didn't mean they were compatible. She knew from experience that loving Travis was not enough to keep them together, that it wouldn't be long before they'd be at one another's throats. And Sandy didn't want a life filled with strife and arguments. She wanted peace and harmony.

With a sigh of resignation, she pulled back from Travis's arms. "The wind is picking up. We have to deal with the rigging."

"And don't forget to stow the bomb in the life raft," Jim told them, reminding her the line was still open. At least it wasn't a picture phone. But she imagined the man knew they'd been in one another's arms. At least he couldn't know how hungry she was to hold Travis, how, right now, she'd rather be with him more than anyone else in the world.

"We'll get right on it. Thanks for the help." Travis turned off the phone and replaced it in the dry box.

While Travis dealt with the deactivated bomb, she surveyed the damage. The mast had snapped away clean, but was dragging behind them in a tangle of stays and shrouds. The easiest thing to do would be to just cut it loose. But before she did so, she examined what was left for them to work with.

An eight-foot section of mast remained, but without

the rigging to support it, with the deck and keel weakened about the base, she suspected it wouldn't hold any kind of sail. They could reinforce supports with the materials floating in the water, repair the fiberglass with a quick-drying patch. But already the hurricane's eye was passing. The sky was darkening again, the light gray deepening to an angry hue of charcoal. And while the sea remained inky black, the swells began to once again increase in size.

She helped Travis launch the dinghy with the americium lashed down tight. For a moment, she feared the dinghy might tangle with the rigging, but then the wind and waves took it away. Deactivated, the bomb could hurt no one, unless it fell into the wrong hands. However, with the U.S. Navy tracking the GPS signal, she had no fears on that account. The military would recover the radioactive elements and investigate the stolen bomb. Hopefully, new procedures and regulations would prevent the same thing from happening again.

All her fears were focused on keeping them afloat for the next few hours. "Travis, if we can winch up some of the rigging, we can use it to support the mast."

"What are you thinking?"

"Suppose we cut a smaller second mast from the remains of the original one, wedge it down into the keel and lash it tight to the base," she suggested, knowing their options were limited. They had about fifteen minutes, maybe thirty, to find a way to stabilize the boat and prevent her from turning broadside into the heavy seas.

Travis surveyed the rigging, then the damaged deck. "What's going to support the mast?"

"We tie lines from the masts to the cleats and the handrails."

"Cleats and handrails aren't meant to take that kind of pressure."

"I know. But do we have another alternative?" she asked, glad he hadn't laughed outright at her suggestion, because she didn't see another option.

"Let's do it."

Twenty minutes later, they had two masts shoved down into the keel. While she tied them together with lines, Travis ran more lines from the mast to the cleats and handrails. With no way to attach a sail to the mast, they simply wound a larger sail around the mast, leaving only a small triangle sticking out. The trick was to use the minimum amount of sail to stabilize it while putting the least amount of pressure on the damaged boat.

With the sea spraying them, a fiberglass patch was impossible to create, so they stuffed an extra sail into the hole to keep out water. When Sandy finally sat in the cockpit and once again held the tiller, she was surprised to see that although the boat was sluggish, she was responsive.

"You know, if the back side of the hurricane isn't as strong as the front," Travis told her, "we're going to make Vanderpelt's island in record time."

"So what's the plan?" she asked him, curling into his side. She hadn't thought much past getting there. But as usual, Travis had the bigger picture in mind.

"You limp in with the boat. If anyone asks, tell them I fell overboard in the storm."

"And where will you be?"

"I'll swim ashore, find Ellie and release her."

She refrained from asking what he would do if Ellie was in no condition to walk. One step at a time. First, he had to swim through the icy water, land undetected on the island and find Ellie. "Are we going to coordinate with Kincaid?"

"Yeah. Boats and planes will come in to support us as soon as the storm allows."

She hesitated, thinking his plan was daring, but risky. He was swimming in by himself to face an unknown force. "Maybe we should wait?"

"Our best strategy is secrecy and surprise."

"As soon as Vanderpelt steps foot on this boat, he's going to know that his bomb is gone," she reminded him, knowing that he must have a plan for her safety, too.

"That's why I want you to delay as long as possible. Come in slowly. If another boat motors alongside, tell them you fear the hull will collapse from a simple bump."

"And if they refuse to wait?"

"I want you to blow up the boat."

She glanced at Travis's face, her heartbeat kicking into overdrive at the harsh set of his jaw, the fierce expression in his eyes. Maybe she'd heard him wrong, but she doubted it.

"You want me to blow up this boat?"

"Yeah. I'll set everything up for you before I leave."

Chapter Thirteen

As they closed in on Vanderpelt's island, Travis made one last call to Kincaid to coordinate their efforts. Unfortunately, help arriving depended on the weather. Travis couldn't wait—not if he wanted to sneak in during the storm.

He stowed communication gear in a dry box, then prepared to slip into the water. But first he shared one last kiss with Sandy. He hated leaving her alone. But he'd known from the beginning of the voyage that this moment would arrive. However, no matter how much he'd prepared, he hadn't realized how difficult abandoning her would be.

He held open his arms. "Come here."

Even through the dry suit he wore to protect him

from the wet and cold during his long swim ashore, he appreciated how closely she pressed herself to him. She threaded her fingers into his hair and pulled his head down until she locked gazes with him. "You be careful."

"You, too." His hammering heart had nothing to do with the danger each of them was about to face. He'd gone over the plan with her repeatedly, and she knew all the contingency options, including how to signal an S.O.S. on her emergency beacon that the Shey Group would immediately pick up. With planes in the sky and boats on the way, she should be fine.

Yet he couldn't ignore the possibility that Vanderpelt could be unpredictable. He didn't want Sandy to deal with him at all, never mind by herself, but if he was going to rescue Ellie, he had to swim in. The plan was to find Ellie before Sandy had to confront Vanderpelt.

"Travis." Sandy spoke softly, her gaze resolute, her fingers pulling the dry suit hood over his head. "Find Ellie and get away. Don't worry about me. I'll be fine."

God, she was so brave. She didn't want him distracted and thinking about her. But how could he not? He wished they'd made love one more time. He wished he'd told her how much she meant to him. He wished he didn't have to say goodbye.

"Go." She kissed him hard, then stepped back, her eyes wide and determined, her tone edged with fire. "Go, while the fog and rain hide me and the boat."

Travis nodded, placed the rebreather into his mouth and flipped backward over the side. Knowing beforehand that he would have to make this swim, he and

Kincaid had left nothing to chance. Travis had a small, motorized propeller with handles, that the SEALs had developed, which pulled him underwater at around five miles per hour. All he had to do was start the engine, aim the trusty sea scooter and hold on.

Once underwater, he periodically checked his position with a GPS unit. Mostly he wondered how Sandy was doing on the surface, and how difficult finding Ellie would be. Insertion onto the island, where he had only himself to worry about, would be the easy part. Extraction with Ellie might be more complicated.

He'd brought an extra rebreather and dry suit in a pack of equipment attached to his back. Under normal conditions, Ellie was a strong swimmer, but he had no idea what kind of condition his sister would be in. She could be physically sick, weak, injured. And her mental state might be anything from desperate to hopeless to hysterical.

Timing would be critical. Sandy's part was crucial. Hopefully, all the attention of Vanderpelt's men would be focused on her sailing toward the island. And she'd delay her sail over the last few miles for as long as possible.

Travis rechecked his position and carefully chose his landing site. He picked a tiny sliver of sand between huge boulders. The swim between surging waves crashing on rocks would be difficult, but the boulders would keep him hidden from any but the most intense surveillance. Hopefully, he'd be lucky enough to avoid the hourly perimeter patrol, but if necessary he was prepared to take them out. The satellites hadn't spotted any dogs, but he carried a knockout spray just in case.

Travis landed on the beach in slicing rain, tossed his flippers to higher ground and immediately donned boots to protect his feet. Then he peeled off his cumbersome dry suit, wedged his and Ellie's swim gear along with the sea scooter well above the high-tide mark between two rocks and checked his weapons. In addition to two guns, extra ammo and several grenades, he carried a knife at his waist, another at his ankle and a third up his sleeve.

Before Travis headed for the outbuildings near the airstrip, or to the far end of the island by Vanderpelt's main compound, he spared a moment to face the sea, and to check Sandy's progress. He had to wait for her to crest atop a wave before spotting her in the spyglass. Sandy had the perfect excuse to delay her journey and avoid sailing a direct line that would bring her too close to the wind. Doing so would put extra pressure on the damaged mast. Since towing the hull with personal seacraft was out of the question in these kinds of waters, and Vanderpelt didn't keep any large boats on the island, he would have to wait for her to arrive.

Good.

The storm worked in Travis's favor. He encountered only one perimeter patrol that he avoided by ducking behind thick underbrush. Everyone else seemed holed up against the slashing wind and cutting rain.

Staying off the shell road that circled the island, but following it, Travis jogged past downed tree limbs, uprooted plants and one live electric wire that snaked loose in the wind. Despite the weather, he appreciated running on terra firma. He enjoyed the sea but preferred to do battle on land.

He tried the front door to the airport hangar and found it locked down tight. He didn't bother with the main building that housed a seaplane. It was unlikely Ellie would be kept there. Travis proceeded to the more remote outbuildings. The first one was full of tools and parts, and he saw no sign of his sister. The second outbuilding was locked with a chain between two door handles, but he'd come prepared with a chain cutter. Inside, he found lawnmowers, a fuel tank and an arsenal of weapons.

Travis debated blowing up the armory. Vanderpelt might blame an explosion on the storm. But then again, Travis might set off a hornet's nest of activity, and he decided that giving away his presence on the island was too big an advantage to risk.

He also found a golf cart and considered whether or not to ride it to the other end of the island. Sometimes hiding right in the open caused less suspicion than skulking through the bushes. If he rode, he might appear to fit in. Yet, the island was small. Chances were, Vanderpelt's men recognized one another on sight.

Travis decided to make his way on foot. The slicing downpour made jogging through the mud a noisier journey than he would have liked. But he simply couldn't take the time to inch through the muck. So every footstep was a splash of water, followed by a sucking sound as he pulled his boot free to take the next step. Despite the fact that he was wet to the skin, the run kept him warm.

Praying the rain would continue, Travis made good time and finally slowed as he came up to three small outbuildings. One appeared to be a garage, the other two storage sheds. The garage, a one-story building constructed of brick and cement, with one small window, was the sturdiest, and the likeliest prison cell.

When a guard checked the lock, Travis eased back against the wall of the nearby shed, his suspicions intensified. He waited for the man to leave, but the man stood guard in front of the door, lit a cigarette and settled in. Travis needed to create a diversion, but not one large enough to draw the attention of more of Vanderpelt's men.

"Don't move." A gun pressed into Travis's head.

SANDY HAD HER HANDS full sailing the damaged boat. However, when she spied a twenty-five-foot cabin cruiser motoring out to her from the island, she realized that Kincaid's intelligence gathering was far from perfect. Vanderpelt must have hidden the boat under trees or some kind of structure.

She and Travis hadn't planned for anyone to try and meet her at sea, and for a moment, fear tensed the muscles between her shoulder blades. Sandy waved as if she was eager for company, and when the boat pulled alongside, she shouted, "My hull is like an eggshell. Approach with care."

"What's wrong?" one of the men yelled back.

Idiot. She pointed to the mast. "We sustained heavy damage."

"We?"

She shook her head. "I lost Travis, my crewman, in the storm."

"We can tow you in," the other captain offered.

Again she shook her head. "The cleats are holding up my mast. You tie in another line for a tow and she may come apart at the seams."

She had to stall. Give Travis time to find Ellie. Luckily, she had excuses ready. She knew the sea and she knew her boat. And she had the added advantage of knowing what they expected to find hidden in her keel. They wouldn't risk sinking the sailboat when she could limp in to shore on her own.

"All right. We'll escort you. That way, we'll be here for you in case you need assistance."

"Where's Ellie?" she called back. "Vanderpelt promised that if I brought him the boat, he'd let her go."

"We don't know anything about that. You sail in and you can take that up with Mr. Vanderpelt."

Yeah, right. When Sandy sailed in, they'd learn that the bomb was no longer on board. Then Travis might have to rescue Ellie *and* her.

Sandy had always known coming back for Ellie was a risk. But she hadn't hesitated and she didn't regret it now. Travis was out there somewhere, and she put her faith in him.

Meanwhile, Sandy concentrated on sailing. She fell off the wind a bit more, slowing her progress. Two more tacks would use up an additional fifteen minutes. Critical minutes.

Her escort noticed immediately. "Lady, you changed course."

"The mast is slipping. I'm trying to keep her from going down. This isn't a race. We aren't in a rush, are we?"

"Mr. Vanderpelt wants this boat now."

"You want me to sail closer to the wind? Fine." She picked up the line attached to the sail, as if about to obey the order. "But if this sailboat sinks, I'm telling Vanderpelt exactly why I sailed through a hurricane and then sank within sight of his island."

The man waved her off. "Better late than never, lady. Just get her back in one piece."

Sandy swallowed a grin of satisfaction.

DAMN, TRAVIS CURSED at the gun aimed at his head. Had he tripped a motion detector and set off a silent alarm? The rain had masked the other man's footsteps. And his focus on finding Ellie had made him less careful than he should have been.

Travis had faced dangerous situations many times before. He might have been caught, but he was nowhere near out of the game. He still had options. And he would go through every one in order to find a way to get to Ellie.

"Hey, I'm Vanderpelt's new guy," Travis tried to bluff as he looked at the other man out of the corner of his eyes, checking for weakness.

"Turn around slowly. Keep your hands up."

The man had stepped back. Far enough that a kick or punch to knock aside the gun was not a possibility. But the man hadn't called for the guard to come help him, either. He seemed to be assessing Travis as if his own life depended on what he did next. His eyes were steady. He didn't appear surprised to see him or particularly worried, almost as if he'd been out here searching for Travis. He could be one of Vanderpelt's loyal followers, but then again, he might have his own agenda.

Travis could try to disarm the man. He could drop, roll and shoot. Or he could try and talk his way out. He took a chance. "I'm Ellie's brother. I work for the Shey Group."

Travis had hoped to make contact with the Mossad agent. If Kincaid had paved the way for him, going through channels, this man might be the guy who'd helped his sister. Before he tried violence, he gave him an opportunity to identify himself by mentioning the Shey Group.

The other man grinned.

SANDY COULD DELAY no longer. She'd drawn out every second, every mile, down to making the men wait to come aboard while she pretended to use the head. In reality, she was sending Kincaid the S.O.S., their signal that she and Travis had abandoned ship.

Too bad the weather appeared as nasty as ever. The winds still gusted, making her eyes tear. The boat bounced against the dock and rain fell in sheets, leaking through the canvas patch and allowing water to overflow the bilge despite the automatic pump. Within hours, the boat would sink—but not before Vanderpelt's men would board and discover that the bomb was no longer there.

Sandy tossed the signaling device under a bunk cushion and turned to face the intruders. "I hope your boss has insurance."

The two men paid no attention to her. One kneeled by where the false floor used to be while the other shined a flashlight on the spot. "It's not here."

"I told you." Sandy forced aggravation into her tone. "We lost the mast. The last thing Travis did before he went over the side was to help me jury-rig two broken pieces."

The men ignored her theatrics. "You broke through the false floor. Where's the suitcase?"

"Suitcase?" Sandy tried to make her voice sound surprised, but had no idea if she succeeded.

"Mr. Vanderpelt's suitcase was stowed right there."

"By the keel? That's where we had to patch the hull. If anything was there, it may have sunk with the other rigging." Sandy squared her shoulders. "What was in the suitcase? I don't deliver drugs."

One of the men grabbed her by the upper arm. "Lady, you can tell the boss."

Uh-oh. Sandy needed to stall. An extra minute might be crucial. Yanking her arm from his grasp, she grabbed a duffel bag and started to pack. "Gentlemen, this boat is sinking. I need to get my stuff."

"Lady, where you're going you won't need any stuff."

She scowled at him then, and backed up. "What are you talking about? I delivered the boat. Vanderpelt needs to let me see Ellie."

"Oh, you'll be seeing her all right. You'll probably be sharing her cell." The man didn't laugh. He had a scared look in his eyes, as if he didn't want to tell Vanderpelt the bad news. That didn't bode well for Sandy, but her hopes rose at the news that Ellie was here. And still alive.

Vowing to slow their progress any way she could, she ran up the steps and prepared to jump overboard. But one of the men caught her before she could escape. "Oh, no you don't. You're not going anywhere except to see Mr. Vanderpelt. And lady, if you know what's good for you, I'd advise you to talk."

"Why?"

"Because I've seen what he does to ladies who piss him off, and it's not pretty."

Despite herself, Sandy shuddered. And she wondered what kind of hell Vanderpelt had put Ellie through.

MUCH TO TRAVIS'S RELIEF, the man placed his gun back in his holster. "I'm Alan. It's about damn time you got here. It's taken me three years to work my way into Vanderpelt's organization. You better have a damn good plan to get her out without blowing my cover."

"That's no longer necessary. Vanderpelt's dirty bomb has been dismantled."

"The radioactive material?" Alan asked, his eyes bright and curious.

"The U.S. Navy should have recovered it by now."

"All right. Let me take care of the guard. He knows me and won't suspect a thing."

"Thanks. And I appreciate you doing what you could for Ellie. You ever need a favor, I owe you." The two men shook hands.

"You've got one spunky sister. She spat in Vanderpelt's face."

Travis wanted to see her with his own eyes. He wanted to get her out of here. But he needed to know what Alan required of him. "Are you staying undercover?"

"Yes."

"This island is going to be taken over by the U.S. Navy and Coast Guard as soon as the storm clears."

The Mossad agent winked at him. "I'll be detained with the others and perhaps learn a few more of their secrets before I escape."

"I understand. Now, let's go get Ellie."

Travis watched Alan walk right up to the guard. He said something Travis couldn't hear and the other man turned and opened the lock, then Alan hit him on the temple with his gun. The guard slumped, and Alan shoved the unconscious body inside the shed and motioned Travis to join him.

Alan and Travis entered the dark cell. "Ellie?"

"Travis!"

Ellie stumbled over the mattress and into his arms. "Alan tossed the guard's body in here and then told me you'd arrived, but I feared it was another of Vanderpelt's tricks."

He hugged her tightly, ignoring the lump in his throat, the tears of relief threatening to spill down his cheeks. "It's no trick. I'm here." He forced back his feelings. That could wait until she was really safe. "Can you walk?"

"Yes. But do you have anything to eat? A candy bar? Mints? Alan tried to sneak me food, but Vanderpelt hasn't fed me in a while, and I don't want to collapse on you."

He shoved two PowerBars into her hands. "Can you eat as we go?"

She unwrapped one and shoved it into her mouth. "Sure."

"Go slow," he warned. "Or it will all come back up."

Alan stepped inside the room, making it crowded. "I need you to tie me up."

Travis understood. Alan needed to look as if he'd been surprised by the enemy, along with the guard. The guard hadn't seen who had hit him, and Alan would be believed.

Travis did the honors, leaving the man as comfortable as he could on his side. Alan raised his head and stared at Ellie as if taking one last precious look. "Good luck, my friends."

Ellie kneeled and kissed Alan. "You'd better call me to tell me you are safe."

He nodded, and then Travis took Ellie's hand and stepped into the rain. "Come on. We need to run a few hundred yards to get out of sight. Don't save any strength. Use whatever you have now. Got it?"

"Oh, God. Travis, is Sandy here with you?"

"Why?" His heart pounded at the fear in Ellie's tone. She looked thin, but seemed mentally sound.

"Because Vanderpelt's men are marching some woman up to the house at gunpoint. I can't tell from here who she is…."

"It's Sandy. I'm getting you out of here and then I'll come back for her."

"We can't leave her to that bastard."

Travis agonized over the only two women in the world he loved. Had he just exchanged Sandy's life for Ellie's?

Chapter Fourteen

Vanderpelt stared at his men, and the woman they were escorting to his office. He would have met the boat at the dock except he'd just gotten some disturbing news from a mole buried deep inside the American bureaucracy. The U.S. Coast Guard had commandeered the second boat at Lighthouse Red. It would be a matter of hours, a day at best, until they found his bomb secreted in her keel.

And since two of his men had been captured, he could assume the overzealous federal agents might find a lead back to him. He had to speculate his cover had been compromised. If he couldn't deliver at least one bomb, four years of work had just dried up like a drop of water in the desert.

Ah, what a coup it would have been to steal bombs from the infidel, dirty them with machines of their own making and explode them over east and west coast metropolitan areas. Tens of thousands would die immediately, hundreds of thousand more, maybe millions, would suffer radiation burns and cancer.

Even better, the army sent to subjugate his people—paid for by the recovering American economy—would be recalled to defend the homeland. The stock market would enter a tailspin and, in an election year, the aggressive American president would lose the vote. The American people were weak from their riches. They would lose heart.

His plan was grand. But he'd known all along the risks, and he'd prepared accordingly. Sometimes it was better to retreat and live to fight another day than to give one's life foolishly.

He would have left an hour ago—risked flying out during the storm. Radar had picked up planes and boats heading his way. Escape must be immediate. And yet, the American woman had somehow survived her voyage and sailed here. Her boat was damaged, but he cared only about its contents. One bomb was better than none.

So he'd delayed his departure and ground his teeth in frustration as she'd limped in like a wounded bird. Picking up his binoculars, he peered through the driving rain toward his men. He saw no briefcase. No smiles. Their heads bowed to wind and rain, his men had dejection and failure written all over their demeanors.

Anger surged through him like a sword. If the American woman had failed, she would pay the consequences for her actions. Her death would not be easy or come quickly. He would enjoy making her suffer along with her friend she'd come to save.

Vanderpelt waited for his men to bring her to him, waited for an explanation that didn't matter. He already knew he'd failed. And yet, he couldn't give up his ambition—not without hearing exactly what had transpired.

His men thrust her into his office and retreated. Like the other American, she had no modesty. Her face and arms were bared, her head held high, her eyes glittering. He would enjoy taming that attitude.

"Where's my bomb?"

"Where's Ellie?" she countered, as if he didn't hold all the cards.

Vanderpelt didn't have time for games. If she'd hidden the bomb, submerged it because she expected a double cross, he had to find out soon—before the American Coast Guard arrived.

"You will join your friend," he promised, his voice silky, "just as soon as you tell me where you hid the bomb."

"I'll tell you the same thing I told your men. There is no bomb. If you hid something between the mast and the keel, it may have sunk into the ocean when the boat pitchpoled—"

"Pitchpoled?"

"Turned bow over stern. In case you haven't noticed, there's a hurricane out there."

"I don't want to hear excuses."

"I wasn't giving you one. If you tampered with the

boat and the bomb fell out, it was the fault of your workers not to make the hull strong. My job was to sail the boat here. I did that."

He believed she'd known nothing about the bomb. And it was likely the story she told was the truth. After all, she was shaking, and he didn't think it was from the cold. She might be standing with her head high, all proud and defiant, but she would learn humility. She would learn to beg. He would enjoy teaching these American women what it was like to serve a man.

"Your job was to deliver my cargo. You failed." There was no more time to get her to talk. That would have to wait. Vanderpelt yelled for his guards. "We're leaving. Now. Get the other woman and meet us in the garage."

He grabbed Sandy by the arm and dragged her to the garage. "Let us go," she said. "We'll only slow you down."

He backhanded her across the face, splitting her lip. Blood welled. She gasped, but didn't cry out. He paid her no more attention, thrusting her into the back seat of his car and climbing in beside her. The idea of the American women sitting on both sides pleased him.

But when the guard came pounding back in, his face worried, Vanderpelt had a bad feeling. "What?"

"Alan is tied up. The other man is unconscious. The American woman is gone."

Damn her. She must be hiding on the island, but he had no time to search. It was possible she'd had help. Perhaps one of his men had even helped her.

"Did Alan say if she had help?"

"He said he can't remember what happened due to the bump on his head."

Vanderpelt let out a roar of frustration. Nothing was working out the way he'd planned. "Drive. Get me out of here. Have the pilot ready the plane."

TRAVIS DIDN'T WASTE a moment, half carrying, half leading Ellie toward the other end of the island where he'd stashed the gear. Ellie tried valiantly to keep up, but she was weak, out of breath and exhausted. The idea of shoving her into a dry suit and sending her out into the rough ocean by herself seemed stupid. But what choice did he have?

He couldn't leave Sandy back there to face Vanderpelt.

"So what's the plan?"

"I hid a dry suit, an air rebreather and a sea scooter, but I'm having second thoughts." Travis sighed to relieve the tension in his neck and back. He'd brought the dry suit to fit the sister he remembered, not the skinny woman, weakened by captivity, who was having trouble standing. "You aren't strong enough to swim."

"Exactly what am I swimming to?" Ellie asked. She might be weak, but her mind was churning on all cylinders.

"Sandy signaled an S.O.S. The navy should be arriving soon."

"How soon?"

"That depends on the weather."

Ellie picked up the dry suit. "Help me into this."

"But—"

"At least I'll be warm." She was shivering, her lips

blue, but the determination in her eyes made him realize she was thinking more clearly than he was.

Sandy's safety consumed all his thoughts. Given enough time, any agent could be made to talk. Lack of sleep and food, enough pain—everyone had a breaking point. And Sandy wasn't a trained operative taught to anticipate what might happen. She didn't know that she should give up the unimportant information, mislead rather than lie.

She was a brave woman. His friend.

He realized too late that they had always been friends. Whether they'd been fighting or loving, they'd kept that friendship. And he damn sure didn't want to lose her. But Ellie was pitifully weak, and leaving her alone might make Sandy's sacrifice for naught.

At the sound of a car's engine, he and Ellie ducked deeper into the cover of the boulders. After the car passed, Travis peered over the rock. Lightning flashed, and he saw Sandy sitting in the back seat, flanked by two men. Vanderpelt had obviously figured out that his operation was blown. Maybe he'd spotted the navy planes or boats on radar. Whatever his reasons, he was escaping. Taking Sandy with him.

Vanderpelt's swift move limited Travis's options. He'd wanted to take Ellie someplace safe, get her aboard a Coast Guard vessel, then return for Sandy. But the cavalry had yet to arrive.

Travis pieced together the Velcro tabs at the wrists of her dry suit. "Ellie, stay on the beach, in the lee of these rocks."

"Okay."

"If anyone except me or the U.S. Coast Guard arrives, dive into the water and hide."

"For how long?" she demanded.

"Until I come back."

She could have asked what to do if he didn't come back. But bless her, she didn't. Instead she hugged him, then shoved him after Sandy. "Go get her."

Ellie had always been intuitive about people. In the short time since he'd rescued her, she'd seemed to somehow know that his concern for Sandy was driven by deep feelings. Love.

Now was not the time.

Travis had to keep his wits about him. This end of the island had one way to escape—the seaplane. The pilot would have to be desperate or crazy to attempt to reach sufficient airspeed to achieve flight in these kinds of waves, in this kind of wind.

But as Travis raced down the road, he saw that his guess had been correct. Two men unlocked the hangar and rolled out a small seaplane.

SANDY'S EARS RANG FROM the blow to her face. Her lips stung, and blood leaked into her mouth. Chills of fear scampered down her spine, making her tremble so that she hugged herself. She didn't want to die on this stinking island. Worse was the thought of Vanderpelt forcing her onto that plane.

She willed her panic to the corners of her mind and focused on escape. Vanderpelt grasped her arm tightly, but she thought she might be able to lunge free. Then what?

Between his driver and the men rolling the seaplane toward a horseshoe-shaped, protected bay that kept back most of the sea's waves, she saw no place to run where they wouldn't immediately catch her. She considered trying to get back into the car and locking the doors, but one of his men had the keys.

Remain alert.

Don't give up.

The men wheeled the seaplane down a short ramp and then pulled it close to a dock with a line. If Vanderpelt took her out on the dock to get her into the plane, she would fling herself free and dive into the water. He might shoot her. One of his men might catch her. But she decided that making the effort would be her only chance. Because once he got her into that plane, she might as well be in a jail cell.

With Vanderpelt's hand gripped on her arm, she tried to stay relaxed. Her tensing muscles could warn him that she was up to something, and her chance of success was better if she took him by surprise.

Sandy wished she had a better plan. She and Travis hadn't expected Vanderpelt to leave the island so quickly. They'd figured she could stall him until Travis could return for her. They'd been wrong.

And yet, even as scared as she was right now, she would make the same choice again. What good could the rest of her life have been if she'd failed to find the courage to go after Ellie?

Sandy didn't want to die. She looked forward to many more days sailing the sea, and spending time with Travis—now there was a dream. During this trip they'd bonded in ways that had shown her that neither of them was the same person they'd once been. She was no longer out to prove her independence. She knew who she was, and giving in to Travis occasionally didn't lessen her self-esteem. And he had matured in ways too many to define. He still had a temper but he controlled it, it didn't control him. And the caring, loving man he'd always been had emerged to make her proud.

Just thinking about him gave her courage. And when Vanderpelt tugged her onto the dock, she had to force her feet to drag, as if she were reluctant, not eager. She kept her breathing normal, giving him no reason to pay the slightest attention to her.

She waited until they were opposite the plane's door. Waited until he started to turn. And then she lunged.

Flung herself into the air.

And dived into the water.

Already wet to the skin from the rain and cold, she didn't expect the icy water to shock her, but it did. Her lungs tightened, and it took a moment to start her legs kicking and her arms pulling her through the water. Holding her breath as long as she could, she headed away from the dock into deeper water. There was no point in heading to land where Vanderpelt's men could simply run around the shoreline and recapture her.

Even before she came up for air, she felt the reverberation in the water behind her. Someone had come after her. Her air-starved lungs burned but she forced herself farther. This was not like swimming in a pool in a sleek swimsuit. Her clothes and shoes weighed a ton, hampering her movements and pulling her downward.

When her lungs demanded that she inhale, she fought to the surface, gulped a breath and slipped right back under. But she'd heard shouts. They'd spotted her.

Sooner or later, they'd catch her.

But she hoped to make coming after her so difficult that it wasn't worth the effort of a man trying to escape the island with his life. Unfortunately, she'd underestimated the swimming strength of her pursuer.

A hand grabbed her ankle. Panicking, already weak from her desperate exertion, she tried to kick loose. And failed. His other hand grabbed the back of her neck and forced her to surface.

Her head cleared the surface and she gasped in air, spit out water and tried to kick at the man holding her. He was too powerful, and when the saltwater cleared from her eyes, she saw that she hadn't swum as far as she'd thought. It took just two minutes for him to wind an arm around her throat and force her back to Vanderpelt, where his men heaved her onto the dock, then into the plane.

With space in the plane limited, and her clothes soaking wet, she didn't merit a seat. Vanderpelt forced her to sit on the floor, then left her to his men to guard while he took the pilot's seat.

Sandy told herself to lunge for the door, but her effort was feeble. She'd spent the last of her energy and her dwindling hope on her swim. Shivering, soaked, she huddled miserably, hugging her knees to her chest.

She reminded herself that the Coast Guard had planes and radar. Surely they wouldn't allow Vanderpelt to get away? She tried, and failed, to submerge her fear that the navy would force down this plane. Or there would be a shootout and she'd be caught in the crossfire.

She knew for certain that the chances of her seeing Travis again didn't look good. And that hurt more than she'd ever thought possible.

TRAVIS HATED LEAVING ELLIE, but once he'd spotted Sandy in Vanderpelt's car, new resolve and strength burst through him. Running on pure adrenaline, he sprinted for the makeshift airport. The road was muddy but it was the fastest route. Drenched from the rain, he barely felt the biting cold. He focused on breathing, on steadily keeping the brutal pace while he made a plan.

He'd already ditched his backpack with most of his weaponry. But he remained armed, determined and dangerous. He went over in his mind the buildings he'd seen earlier. Betting Vanderpelt would take the straightest course from the seaplane's hangar to taking off in the protected harbor, Travis changed his position, angling toward the dock.

He cleared a rise to see Sandy fling herself into the water. Proud that she was still fighting, worried that they might shoot her, furious that they were unwilling to permit her escape, he forced his tired legs to run faster. Sandy's efforts had bought him precious seconds to reach her, but even as he saw a man follow, catch her and force her back to the dock, he knew his timing would be close.

He couldn't go in shooting. Not with them holding Sandy between them like a shield. When Vanderpelt shut the seaplane's door and started the engines, Travis redoubled his efforts. With his gaze focused on the seaplane's skis—and his ultimate goal—he raced onto the dock.

The plane was already moving, but he leaped, caught a strut and held on tight as the small plane labored to reach takeoff speed. With the high winds, the choppy waters and Travis's unexpected weight, he could feel the motor struggling. Reaching up, he yanked open the door, grasped a man who was just rising out of his seat to look out the window and pulled him right out the door into the water.

Sandy glanced at Travis and her face turned stark white. She gasped, as if the shock was almost too much for her to comprehend. But Travis had no time for explanations. Vanderpelt's copilot was heading toward him, gun in hand, just as the plane finally lifted off—no doubt helped by the weight of one less body.

Sandy tripped the copilot, and Travis, keeping hold of the strut with only one hand, drew his gun and shot him. "Come on." He reached out for Sandy as the wind roared in his ears. "We have to get out now."

She crawled toward him and he helped to steady her on the strut. "Oh…my God."

"You can do this. Jump."

"I—"

"Jump!"

She let go. He placed an explosive device on the plane and then he jumped, too.

The fall seemed too quick, the landing too hard. He seemed to go down forever with the water closing over his head, the pressure in his ears requiring him to swallow hard several times. Finally, he reversed direction, praying that Sandy had made it back to the surface on her own. He told himself that she was a strong swimmer, but one glance at her dilated eyes had told him she'd been in shock.

Travis burst back up, and even as he drew his first breaths he scanned the surface for signs of Sandy. Her fall had been slightly shorter than his, but if she'd landed in a belly flop, she could have had the wind knocked out of her, or been knocked out completely. He had to find her fast. She could drown in less than two minutes.

He swam toward the direction he'd seen her last, praying she would pop to the surface. But the gently rolling waves of the harbor mocked him. And when Vanderpelt's plane exploded, he barely glanced at the man's fiery death.

He needed to find Sandy. Soon.

ELLIE KNEW TRAVIS WOULD be furious that she didn't obey his orders to stay put. But she damn well wasn't going to hide in safety when Sandy was in danger and Travis was risking his life to save her. Ellie might still be weak, but the PowerBars had done wonders for her strength and morale. Picking up a gun from Travis's bag, she checked to make sure it was loaded, slipped an extra clip into a pocket, then headed after her brother.

She had no trouble following Travis's deep, running footsteps in the mud. Knowing that she could never keep up with him, she didn't try, especially not in the dry suit that kept her so warm she had to unzip the front to avoid overheating. Instead, she took care to stay on course and to keep her wits about her.

The sound of the airplane motor above the keening wind and rain led her in the right direction. She flicked off the gun's safety and carefully headed down to the water, using brush and trees from the bank to hide her approach.

She couldn't actually see the low-flying plane until she was almost at the beach. And at the sight, her heart almost stopped. Travis was holding on to a strut, opening the door, flinging a man into the water.

She heard a shot, feared her brother or her friend had taken a bullet, saw Sandy, then Travis, fall into the harbor.

Ellie didn't wait to see more. Shoving her gun into the open zipper, she kept her gaze on the spot where Sandy had disappeared. Knowing instinctively that her friend might need her help, and knowing that the dry suit made her buoyant and kept her warm, she swam in sure, swift strokes, praying Sandy would rise to the surface on her own. Because as carefully as Ellie had tried to recall exactly where Sandy plunged in, the water all looked the same.

She saw a hand pop up. Wave. And she headed for

it. Only to realize it was the man Travis had thrown from the plane.

Ellie reached for her weapon. Sandy and Travis were beyond Vanderpelt's man, farther out in the water, and they might be injured. If the man tried to stop her, she vowed to shoot him.

However, he paid no attention to Ellie and swam for shore. Relieved, she flicked the gun's safety back on, replaced the weapon inside her dry suit and kept swimming. When the tiny plane exploded, she had no regrets that Vanderpelt was dead. The bastard deserved to die.

SANDY STRUCK THE WATER at a bad angle. The shock of landing ripped the breath from her lungs. And then she was plunging into the icy depths, her fingers and toes tingling as if lightning had short-circuited her body. She couldn't seem to move. Just blinked, as bubbles of air leaked from her mouth.

After Travis's efforts to save her, she was going to drown. But this was a better death than Vanderpelt would have offered. The sea was pitch dark, beautiful, like inky velvet. Comforting. Safe.

She needn't move. Needn't struggle. This was her time and she could do no more.

After a while she couldn't feel the cold. Tiny stars burst before her eyes, too beautiful to touch. She floated down a long tunnel that swirled with maroon and midnight blues.

There was no pain. Only peace.

She wished Travis could be with her to share this wonderful scenery. And then, somehow, he was there, but his face didn't look serene at all.

Chapter Fifteen

Travis's fingertips touched hair, and he dived deeper, grasped Sandy under the arms and kicked like hell for the surface. Praying it wasn't too late, trying to recall exactly how long she'd been under, he used the last of his adrenaline reserve to take her to the surface. His head, then hers, popped through.

Automatically, he drew in huge lungfuls of air. Sandy didn't. Fearing that he might be too late to start mouth-to-mouth resuscitation if he waited until he reached the shore, he closed her nostrils and breathed into her mouth, but she floated away. He needed four hands—two to hold her afloat, two to keep her still.

He heard the splash of a strong swimmer approaching and debated whether to go for his knife or keep

Sandy's face turned upward to the air. The choice wasn't a difficult one. He maintained his grip on Sandy.

When Ellie's face popped upward, instead of one of Vanderpelt's men, Travis thought he was seeing things. Then he realized she'd disobeyed orders. But he was glad. He couldn't save Sandy by himself, and his sister could help.

"Keep her floating on her back," he told Ellie.

Ellie did as he asked, which allowed him to turn Sandy's head, pinch her nostrils and breathe into her mouth.

"She's not responding." Ellie's voice was grim. "Travis, try again."

He needed no urging, repeating the maneuver while feeling for a pulse. If her heart had stopped, this attempt to start her lungs wouldn't work.

Come on.

"Breathe."

Even as he blew air into Sandy's mouth, he felt a faint pulse in her neck. And then she coughed up seawater and her eyes fluttered open.

"Don't try to talk," he directed. "We'll swim you to shore," he told her, his panic easing as he saw her eyes narrow on him, and a slight nod of her jaw in understanding.

It seemed to take forever to reach the beach, but in reality, it must have taken just minutes. Her hands were so cold, too cold. Her hair was a dripping mess and he couldn't have cared less. She was alive. Responsive. And aware.

As if the sky had used up all its tears, the rain finally

stopped and the clouds scudded away, leaving streaks of orange and slashes of red. The harbor's water took on a deep, beautiful blue, somewhere between cerulean and azure. The sound of rescue-chopper motors reached him long before he spied them in the sky, but his attention was focused on Sandy. She didn't move much, allowing Travis and Ellie to tug her with them. And she wore the most serene expression on her face, almost as if she'd seen a vision.

Travis had been around several men who'd had near death experiences. Each had been different, fascinating and life-altering. One of the Shey Group's mission specialists had become a monk, another had made up with the wife he'd been in the process of divorcing, a third had quit the outfit that day and they'd never heard from him again.

Once they could stand, Ellie and Travis carried Sandy to a grassy spot to lie down. Only, Sandy wanted to sit cross-legged and she grabbed each of their hands and pulled them down beside her.

Puzzled, Travis and Ellie exchanged glances but neither said a word to the other. Instead, Travis turned to Sandy, his tone tight, his heart erratic. "What's up?"

"I thought I was going to drown and I had only one regret." Sandy squeezed his hand and he looked down to see that she was squeezing Ellie's, too.

"Only one?" Ellie's chuckle was cheerful. "I would have had dozens."

"I've never told you both how much I love you." Sandy's voice was warm, firm, her tone loving and powerful. "Too often we go through life and we never tell the people who mean the most to us how we really feel about them. Ellie, I love you for being the best girlfriend I've ever known."

The two women hugged, but Travis didn't release Sandy's hand.

"And Travis, we don't always see eye to eye, but I love you, too. Even as I was dying, a tiny part of me told the rest that you wouldn't let me go. Without your presence in my life, I wouldn't have kept fighting for as long as I did."

"Oh, Sandy." Travis hugged her and their mouths fused, creating heat, creating hope, creating promises for the future.

"Ahem." Ellie cleared her throat. "If you two don't intend to stop, you need to find a room."

When Travis finally broke the kiss, he could see that Ellie was smiling her approval—not that he needed it. Still, it was nice to know that the sister he adored and the woman he loved were best friends. More than best friends. Each had risked her life for the other, creating a bond so tight, he had no doubt it would last a lifetime.

"Damn you, Travis," Ellie cursed him.

He jerked his head around. "What? What did I do wrong now?"

Both women broke into peals of laughter. He glared from one to the other, totally confused. Had they both lost it? Was Ellie going nuts on him after enduring her captivity? And Sandy was rolling on the grass, holding her stomach and laughing so hard that tears trickled from the corners of her eyes.

Finally, Sandy took pity on him. "Ellie, he doesn't have a clue."

"I know…that's what makes…"

"What?" he almost shouted. But he sensed their laughter was embracing him. They weren't laughing so much at him as with him—except he didn't yet get the joke.

Ellie shook her head, leaned forward and kissed him on the cheek. "Brother, dear. When a woman tells you that she loves you, you're supposed to respond."

"I did."

"I didn't hear you say a thing," Sandy contradicted him, her eyes sparkling.

"But I kissed you."

Ellie rolled her eyes. "That's nothing."

"My…kisses…are…not nothing." He frowned at her, finding speaking difficult between teeth clenched in frustration.

Ellie punched him in the shoulder.

"Ow."

"You idiot—"

"Must I remind you—" he eyed his sister as if she was an alien "—I just sailed through a hurricane to save your life?"

"Sandy needs to hear you say the words."

"I just climbed on a taxiing airplane's strut for her."

"Not enough." Ellie shook her head, her lips twitching with a grin.

"I saved her from Vanderpelt."

"Only after she risked her life to help me." Again Ellie shook her head. "Not enough."

"I just breathed life back into her lungs."

"So now you owe me," Sandy took over. "You owe me words."

"Don't you know?"

"I've always known." Sandy's tone was calm, yet giddy.

"Fine." He crossed his arms over his chest, then scowled at Ellie. "You can leave now."

"Oh, no. Not when the conversation is just getting interesting, I'm not. I've been waiting eight years to hear this. Secondhand won't be the same."

"I love her, now scram." He swatted Ellie on the butt. He was sure she didn't feel a thing through the thick dry suit, but nevertheless, she departed, giving them maybe twenty feet of privacy—just enough that their voices wouldn't carry if they kept them low.

"You know, it would have been nice if I'd been the first person you told," Sandy murmured, winding her arms around his neck. "But I'll forgive you."

He raised an eyebrow. "Is that so?"

"Yeah, but only if you tell me again."

"I love you. Of course, that doesn't mean we won't fight."

"Of course."

"But we'll always make up. And we'll always be in love. Deal?"

"Deal."